A-31804

372.64   Pellowski, Anne.
PEL
         The storytelling
         handbook.

$15.00

DATE			
49			
MY 24 '96			

The Storytelling Handbook

A Young People's Collection
of Unusual Tales
and Helpful Hints
on How to Tell Them

ANNE PELLOWSKI

illustrated by Martha Stoberock

SIMON & SCHUSTER BOOKS FOR YOUNG READERS

For Paul, Joey, Jacob, Cameron, Cole, Alexa, and Hannah
—A. P.

For David, Jessica, and Johanna with love
—M. S.

SIMON & SCHUSTER BOOKS FOR YOUNG READERS
An imprint of Simon & Schuster Children's Publishing Division
1230 Avenue of the Americas, New York, New York 10020
Text copyright © 1995 by Anne Pellowski
Illustrations copyright © 1995 by Martha Stoberock
All rights reserved including the right of reproduction in whole or in part in any form.
SIMON & SCHUSTER BOOKS FOR YOUNG READERS is a trademark of Simon & Schuster.
The text for this book is set in Palatino.
The illustrations are rendered in ink.
Manufactured in the United States of America
First Edition
10 9 8 7 6 5 4 3 2 1

Library of Congress Cataloging-in-Publication Data
Pellowski, Anne.
   The storytelling handbook: a young people's collection of unusual tales and helpful hints
on how to tell them / by Anne Pellowski.
      p. cm.
   Includes bibliographical references
   Summary: A guide to storytelling, with a selection of stories from around the world.
   ISBN 0-689-80311-7
   1. Storytelling—Juvenile literature.   2. Storytelling ability in children—Juvenile literature.
[1. Storytelling.   2. Storytelling—Collections.   3. Folklore.]   I. Title.
   LB1042.P434   1995   372.64'2—dc20   95-2991

Contents

Part Two
SELECTING AND PREPARING STORIES TO TELL   21

Part Three
STORIES FOR YOUNG PEOPLE TO TELL   39

iv

Introduction

Storytelling has been going on for a long time. Most of the peoples of the world, from ancient times to the present day, have told stories for one reason or another. We can see what ancient storytellers looked like by studying pictures drawn on walls or sculptures made thousands of years ago. Early writing on papyrus, on cloth, on palm leaf pages, and on animal skins tells us a little about the kinds of stories that were told. In those old records there is only a little information about children and young people telling stories.

In recent years I have met many children and teenagers who are doing storytelling. They have told me about some of the ways they have learned to tell stories, and about the places where they practiced their storytelling skills. They found it hard to explain why they enjoyed storytelling so much, and I could understand that very well. I myself have a difficult time putting into words just why I find storytelling so satisfying, so fulfilling.

Perhaps it is best summed up by twelve-year-old Raven, who said simply, but with deep conviction, "I feel good telling a story." His family came to Canada from Cambodia, and even though English is a second language for him, he enjoys telling stories to the younger children in his school in Toronto.

There are many handbooks and guidebooks for storytellers already in print. Most of them are written for adults. Those books have suggestions that can help you, the young storyteller, as well. But when I am in a school helping students to start storytelling, or to get better at it, there is often one student who will ask, "Isn't there a storytelling book just for us?"

This book is meant to be "just for you." By telling you about some of the young people who have done many different kinds of storytelling, and the variety of places they have told stories, I hope you are inspired to begin (or continue) your own storytelling specialty.

This book is also for you if you want to tell a story but you haven't found the right one to tell. There are many fine books with stories that are good for telling, but each story included in this book was selected especially because a child or young person has told it, or was hoping to tell it in the future.

Most of the young people I interviewed or corresponded with while writing this book said that they liked, best of all, to tell and to listen to stories that had some unusual twist or surprise, either in the action or the ending. That is why I included so many titles of this type in *The Storytelling Handbook*.

Part One

HOW YOUNG PEOPLE CAN
GET STARTED IN STORYTELLING

How did young people
get started in storytelling?

Most of the storytelling done by children and young people started in schools and libraries. In the last century, when schools and libraries were still new, children in all grades performed "recitations" or "monologues" at special times in the year. That is, they recited poems or long speeches from plays or novels or other books.

Your parents and grandparents probably heard stories told in their homes, or in a public library story hour. In the early 1970s storytelling began to appear regularly in quite a few schools. A few key teachers and school librarians began to recognize the enjoyment that storytelling could bring to the classroom. These teachers began to write about their experiences, and to tell other teachers what a wonderful effect storytelling could have on their classes.

Robert Rubinstein, Lynn Rubright, Larry Johnson, Mary Lynne McGrath, Lucille Thomas, and Betty Nicholas are just a few teachers who started unusual storytelling programs that got children interested in listening to stories, and in telling them.

In Eugene, Oregon, Robert Rubinstein started a course for his Roosevelt Middle School students. Soon those students from the first Troupe of Tellers will have their twenty-fifth class reunion!

In Kirkwood, Missouri, near St. Louis, Lynn Rubright, a storyteller and teacher, organized and directed a storytelling project in the elementary schools of Kirkwood. It was called Project Tell, and its purpose was to bring storytelling to all children, as part of the language arts classes.

One of the middle school students at that time was Betsy Boyd. She is now a university student, and she has this to say about her story experience back then: "I am currently majoring in literature—I guess that speaks to my love of language in all forms. Lynn Rubright and the stories she told were a large part of the fostering of my respect. She will always stand out in my memory as someone who brought images and sounds of the Africa that belonged to Anansi, as I sat very small in a classroom very far from anything like that. Telling stories and entertaining is something I have always enjoyed. I think Project Tell and, of course, my very literary, very supportive and wonderful parents, had a hand in that. Someday I hope I can tell my own children stories to fire their imaginations."

Students in the Pillsbury School, part of the Minneapolis Public School system, have been learning to tell stories ever since Larry Johnson became a storyteller in residence there more than a dozen years ago. Under his guidance the students tell stories in their own class. Then they go to other classes to share their stories. They perform outside the school as well.

Did you love pockets when you were little? Maybe you still like them. Mary Lynne McGrath, of the Sacramento City Unified School District, used this love of pockets to get her first and second graders started in storytelling. After hearing a story, each child would draw pictures of the main events in the story. They took their story pictures home in their pockets. Later, they would bring out their Pocket Story and try to tell it to their families.

The following day or week the class would discuss their experiences in telling the story to their families. A number of the children tried out a familiar opening. They said to their parents, in their best pretend voices, "Now if you'll be very good and quiet, I'll tell you a bedtime story."

One of the students said, "I told it to my family when we were at Shakey's Pizza waiting for the pizza to come." Another, a boy from a family originally from Pakistan, said, "I told it in the car to my grandma when we were driving to the Roseville auction. But first I put it in my language. She said she liked it and asked me to tell her all the stories I knew."

The students in Sacramento schools still have Mrs. McGrath to help and inspire them. For more than ten years her Pocket Story technique has been used by many young children in school classes, to get them started in storytelling.

Some school systems started contests or festivals to encourage students to tell stories. One of the first contests took place in New York City. It began in the 1976–1977 school year, and it still takes place today. Soon there will be children in that contest whose parents were in it twenty years ago! That contest was begun by Lucille Thomas, who was in charge of all the city's school libraries at that time. Ms. Thomas felt it was important for young people to learn how to speak smoothly, using correct grammar. She believed that memorizing gave young students a chance to practice good mental discipline. If you are one of the fifty thousand students who enter that contest each year, you will be required to memorize your story.

If you belong to a family with a parent in the military, chances are you have attended one of the Department of Defense Dependent Schools, commonly known as DODDS. They are located all over the world, wherever the United States has large military bases.

Betty Nicholas, the language arts coordinator for the DODDS school in Germany, has directed a Storytelling and Oral Reading Festival for the past eight years. All children in fifth grade participate in oral reading and all children in sixth grade do storytelling. Each grade selects its best reader and storyteller, and the school nominates one reader and one storyteller to take part in regional presentations. A few students are then chosen from each region to go to the national festival, which is usually held in April.

Those are just a few examples of places where children and young people have been telling stories for quite a few years.

Where and when
you can tell stories now

In a school or library

If you want to start storytelling in your class, ask your teacher if you can do it as part of language arts. In schools that allow you to do independent study, you could make up a contract to give a half-hour storytelling program to all of the children in kindergartens and first grades in your school system. By telling the same stories to several groups of children, you will be getting lots of practice and probably learn more about yourself as a storyteller than you can learn in any class or from any book.

The next time you have to do a special report on a country and you want to make it interesting to the class, don't just tell facts—tell a story as well. Rebecca Stallings once did that in her sixth-grade class in Oklahoma."I had to do a report on Sweden," she said,"and so I told the story 'The Squire's Bride.'" Later, she wrote a poem about her experience. (See page 108.)

If you want to know whether your school has ever had student storytelling clubs or festivals or contests, ask the librarian or teacher who has been there the longest time. Perhaps your interest will help to revive an activity that stopped because a key teacher or librarian moved away.

Does your school hold assembly programs or talent shows at special times of the year? When Cheryl Sawyer was thirteen years old, she decided to tell "The Three Bears" at the talent show—but not in English, in Finnish! She did not win any prizes at the talent show, but so many people heard about her unusual telling, she was asked to repeat her story at ethnic festivals throughout Wisconsin. Now she gets paid to tell in schools in Minnesota and Wisconsin. She tells other stories, but the audience favorite is still "The Three Bears" in Finnish.

When the Toronto Board of Education inaugurated a new president, the inauguration program included many musical groups from schools in the city. Another highlight was the African storytelling session re-created by three students of Sprucecourt School. They learned to tell stories in their special classes with Ruth Johnson. Mrs. Johnson has found that many of the children who especially like storytelling are those who are not good in sports or music or academics. Storytelling gives them a chance to show their skills in public, just like the athletes and musicians in the school do.

At the annual potluck dinner for the entire Sprucecourt School community, four children told different parts of the Sedna story, a tale found in many different versions among the Inuit of Canada. They were students in Mrs. Johnson's English as a second language class, and learned to tell stories there.

These students' families are originally from Afghanistan, Somalia, and Vietnam. In those cultures marriages are often arranged. One of these students said she liked telling the story of Sedna because, "Sedna gets to pick her own husband and I want to pick my own husband when I grow up."

In a forensics club

In forensics clubs students practice playacting, debating, oral interpretation (reading aloud), storytelling, and many other types of public speech performance. In each category students are encouraged to perform at the school, the subdistrict, the district, and the state levels. In the storytelling category each student must usually be prepared to tell three stories, one for each of three subjects. At performance time each student picks a slip out of a box, and the slip tells which subject the story must fit.

When Riza Falk of Fountain City, Wisconsin, performed as a freshman in the storytelling category, she had to be prepared with stories that fit these subjects: ghosts, animals, European folktales. As a ghost story she chose "Tailypo," and for the animal story, "Who's in Rabbit's House?" But at the state level she pulled out the slip for European folktales, so she told "The Old Traveler," a tale from Estonia found in *The Moon Painters and Other Estonian Folktales*.

Find out if your school has a forensics club. Such clubs are active in many junior and senior high schools, especially in the Midwestern states.

In a storytelling club

If you are inspired to form a troupe such as the one organized by Robert Rubinstein in Eugene, Oregon, see if your librarian or teacher can get a copy of the videotape *When the Troupe Tells Tales* (see bibliography). On that videotape you will see and hear how some of the members of that troupe perform.

Check in your public library to find out if they have a storytelling club or group. The Traveling Storytellers is another storytelling club that you may want to model yours on. It was started by Stephanie Gildone, the children's librarian at the Conneaut Carnegie Library in Conneaut, Ohio. She saw the interest that young people had in storytelling, so she organized a workshop. Eighteen of the young people who attended enjoyed the experience so much they formed a group called The Traveling Storytellers. Together, the group studied some of the old folktales, searching for one they would all enjoy telling.

"When someone mentioned 'Rapunzel,' we all liked it right away," said Abby Laughlin, a group member. "The first three letters, R A P, gave us the idea of writing a 'rap' based on that story." Jennifer Johnston, another member of the group, found that, "The hardest part of the rap was getting the words to rhyme and memorizing it. A few of my favorite lines are:

> *When Rapunzel was twelve the witch put her in a tower*
> *Which had no doors, steps, or flowers.*
> *Each evening the mean old witch would say*
> *In her mean old, mean old witchy way*
> *"Rapunzel, Rapunzel, will you please let down your hair!*
> *Rapunzel, Rapunzel, and let me climb that golden stair."*

Later, the group wrote a story about what happened after Rapunzel and the Prince married. (See page 105.)

The Traveling Storytellers of Conneaut performed in many schools in their area. Josh Williams, a thirteen-year-old teller in the group, said the best part was, "the look on the children's faces. . . . I enjoyed their curiosity, smiles, and most of all their laughter. . . . Being in the group gave me confidence and courage to speak and act in front of other groups."

As a baby-sitter or child minder

If you've ever had to baby-sit a younger brother or sister, or if you baby-sit for money, you may already know that storytelling can be a useful skill. Young children usually sit up and pay attention when a story is told. Jane K., who baby-sits in the Brown Deer, Wisconsin, area, finds that her stories told with nesting dolls have a special appeal. She makes up the stories, often using the children she is watching as characters in the tales. She also likes to tell handkerchief stories, especially "Mouse Story" and "Rabbit Story." (See *The Family Storytelling Handbook* in the bibliography) "Afterward," says Jane, "I always notice the little kids trying to fold the handkerchief the way I did, but it doesn't work for them. But they keep on trying, and ask me to show them again and again."

Jocelyn Lippert learned storytelling from her mother, Meg Lippert, a professional storyteller and writer who lives in the state of Washington. She uses her story skills so effectively as a baby-sitter that she was once offered a job from a complete stranger, on a beach in Hawaii, where she was on vacation. A mother observed Jocelyn playing with children, and she hired her on the spot to do baby-sitting.

Melissa McCulloch of New Jersey likes telling trick stories to surprise and delight the children for whom she baby-sits. One of her stories, "The Fisherman's Surprise," can be found later in this book.

At a camp or during a sleep-over

Hundreds of children and young people have told me that they first heard stories told at a camp. Most of them remembered at least one of the spooky or silly stories they had heard. It was usually camp counselors or other adults who had told the spooky stories. Very few children or young people could remember hearing really scary stories told by someone their own age. It seems as though, for a story to raise goose bumps on your skin, you really have to hear it from an adult with a lot of campfire storytelling experience.

Young campers often tell hilariously funny and downright silly stories the most. When Abby N. and her Girl Scout troop in Milwaukee go on sleep-overs, their favorite way of telling silly stories is to pass around a stuffed gorilla toy. Whoever ends up with the gorilla at the end of one story is supposed to tell the next story. The gorilla has to be included in the story!

Mike, Dave, and John Collard, who attended camps in the Cleveland, Ohio, area for many years, remember the wild and wacky stories told by Michael Mannen, Larry Sack, and his brother, Jim Sack. "I can still hear Michael telling the story of the 'falumphmaker,'" says Dave. "He would drag it out with all sorts of exaggerations, and in the end this thing taking years to be made by two hundred men using one hundred thousand tons of steel, and so on, would land in Lake Erie with a 'falumph.'"

A few of these funny and far-out tales can be found in *American Children's Folklore,* compiled by Simon J. Bronner.

Some young people try to tell stories that the audience finds "yucky" or "gross." At a school in Tucson a fifth grader mentioned that he had learned a spitting story at camp, but he did not want to tell me the whole story because, he said, "it would gross you out." Most of these stories seem to be told in secret, when adults are not listening. Adults tell this kind of story, too, and they usually like to do it when no children are around. Jan Harold Brunvand has collected some stories of this type. They can be found in *The Vanishing Hitchhiker, The Choking Doberman, The Baby Train,* and other books by him.

At a community festival or event

Schools and libraries are not the only places to find storytelling festivals. Many cities and towns have them in parks, tents, theaters, auditoriums, and other public places. If you would like to appear at such a festival, check with the organizers to see if they offer a specific program in which children and young people get to show off their storytelling talents.

The St. Louis Storytelling Festival, held under the Arch each year, has such a program slot. Ruthilde Kronberg has guided a number of young people through their first appearances at the festival, where the audiences can be quite large. Christine Wiegand, age thirteen, likes to tell humorous stories, and she got her chance to do so at the 1992 and 1993 festivals. Mona Vespa, age twelve and another teller at the same two festivals, says, "My favorite kinds of stories for telling are ones that have good morals, stories that have happened, and stories with lots of character." For the festivals she selected folktales with those qualities. However, she finds the audience responds enthusiastically to any kind of story that is well told.

Larry Johnson's students from the Pillsbury School in Minneapolis perform at all sorts of community festivals and celebrations. Here is a list of a few of them:

Winter Solstice Concert—*Ramsey International Arts Center*
Remembrance Days—*Lake Harriet Peace Garden*
Summer Celebrations—*Children's Museum of St. Paul*

Mother's Day Festival—*Gibb's Farm*
Great Groundhog's Day Get-together—*KFAI Radio*
Metronet Regional Library Meeting
Regional Reading Association Conference

Some of the students, among them Stacy Larkins, Agniezka Czechowicz, and Sarah Burman, performed regularly at restaurants and bookstores in the area. This listing can perhaps give you an idea of places to offer your storytelling talents in your community.

As a professional performer

Some young people get paid for telling stories. Most of them got started because one of their parents is a professional teller. Diane Wolkstein began her career telling stories at the Hans Christian Andersen statue in Central Park, New York. Her daughter, Rachel Zucker, usually went along to listen to the story sessions. Diane often invites audience members to share any stories they have, and one summer when she was about six, Rachel whispered to her mother, "Can I go next, Mom?" She closed her eyes and told "Squirrel's Song" beautifully, without a hitch. After that, Rachel asked to tell other stories now and then. Occasionally, she and Diane performed in tandem.

Rachel is now a graduate student, and uses her storytelling skills in her part-time work at a day care center. But most of all she loves to use her camera to capture the special moments of her mother's storytelling.

Jean Greenwood, who tells professionally in the Wausau, Wisconsin, area, began including her daughter Molly in some of her story performances from the time Molly could speak clearly. At first, Molly just helped in holding up puppets and other objects, but now she is ten and a full-fledged storyteller. Molly has performed alone, but mostly she and her mother work in tandem. Her favorite story is "Max's Christmas."

Meg Lippert, a professional storyteller and writer, has two daughters, Jocelyn and Dawn. Both of them have performed professionally with their mother. Jocelyn, age eleven, writes, "In October I told stories with my mother at a Halloween festival at an herb farm near where we live. My mom dressed as a witch and I was her black cat. In one day we gave eleven storytelling performances. At the end we were both exhausted, but it was really fun. At our forty-five-minute lunch break we got to eat with the employees and go into the Employees Only areas. It made me feel very special. Sometimes I tell stories with my mother and my little sister. We often tell the same stories that we tell with two of us, but we change them to be told by three people. We tell at all kinds of places. I like telling at schools the most because afterward kids sometimes ask us for our autograph!"

Dawn Lippert, age nine, has performed with her mother in many places. She writes, "My mom and I were storytelling in Texas about a year ago. We told around the Fort Worth area. I have also done storytelling in Seattle and other places in Washington, in New York, Maine, and Massachusetts. I like to get paid when I do storytelling; it's one of my favorite parts."

If you do not have a parent who is a professional teller but would like to get a start as a paid performer, begin by volunteering to tell stories at birthday parties, to young Scouting groups, and at other places where people are looking for different kinds of entertainment. If you are a good storyteller, you will soon be getting requests to perform for groups that pay a small fee.

Some children and young people hear storytelling for the first time at the religious center where they are learning about their family's religion. Religious education programs of all types often use stories to pass on the history and beliefs of that particular faith.

Unitarians use a lot of stories from all the world's religions in their Sunday school programs for children. They believe it is important for children to be familiar with many belief systems. Molly Greenwood, whose mother is religious education director at a Unitarian church in Wausau, Wisconsin, helps her mother in storytelling during the Sunday school sessions. As mentioned before, they also perform professionally, and get paid for it, but Molly volunteers her time for her church. Molly says, "I like telling to the younger classes because they laugh a lot and ask you questions, but the older kids sort of just look at you."

Josh Williams of Conneaut, Ohio, called on his experience in story-telling with The Traveling Storytellers to help his mother in the religious education program of their church. "My mom teaches a kids' program for three- to four-year-olds," said Josh. "It's a Peace Program. The pastor's wife works with the parents and my mom is in charge of the little kids. I told some stories and then on the last day, as a surprise for the kids, I came in full costume as a clown. The kids loved it. It was the suggestions from the Storytelling Workshop [in the Conneaut Carnegie Library] that made me brave enough to be in front of those kids."

Ruth Stotter, a storyteller and teacher from California, first remembers seeing and hearing actual storytelling while she was attending a national meeting of B'nai B'rith Girls. She was thirteen at the time. There was a session during which different girls could show off their talents, and one of the girls told a story in which she used a very dramatic Hebrew chant that is part of the Yom Kippur services. "It made me all shivery," says Ruth, "and I said to myself, Next time I come I am going to tell a story like that."

A few years ago I helped the Medical Mission Sisters in Philadelphia celebrate by having a program of stories related to the holidays associated with the winter solstice: Saturnalia, old Scandinavian Jul, Hanukkah, Christmas, Divali, and others. At one point members of the audience were invited to come up and share their stories. Luke Schwarz and Colin Di Garbo were among the children who stood up and told stories about the personal meaning Christmas has for them.

At home among the family

The easiest place to tell stories is at home, to someone in your family. There, you don't have to worry about whether you are doing everything just right. And, as one of the students in Sprucecourt School in Toronto said, "Telling a story can change you from a bad mood to a good mood."

Sometimes a story read in a book at school seems just right to share at home. During the winter of 1993–1994, when it was so cold and snowy and icy in Connecticut, Kathryn discovered *50 Below Zero* by Robert Munsch. That seemed just the perfect story to share at home with her family, to give them a laugh and show them that it could be worse!

In the spring of 1992, while on my way to Frankfurt, Germany, I noticed a girl of about ten sitting across the aisle in the plane. She was entertaining her little sister with handkerchief stories. "Where did you learn those stories?" I asked her. "I was at my grandma's house, and she showed me how to do them," answered the girl. "She found them in a book at the library."

I like to think that the stories were learned from one of my earlier books, *The Family Storytelling Handbook.* And my wish is that someday in the future I will be in a home, in a school or library, or maybe on a plane again, and hear some young person telling a story from this book.

Part Two

SELECTING AND PREPARING
STORIES TO TELL

Finding a good story to tell

Some say that the hardest part of storytelling is finding a good story to tell. I agree. Until I found a fairly large number of stories that I really liked and wanted to tell, I never seemed to have the right story for the right occasion.

However, only a few of the young people I talked to seemed to agree that this was the hardest part of storytelling. Many of them said they found stories they liked fairly easily. Most of them were directed to the stories they told by teachers, librarians, parents, or professional storytellers. Dawn Lippert, age nine, who tells professionally with her mother, Meg Lippert, actually finds that story searching is fun! She writes: "My favorite part about storytelling is learning new stories and deciding which ones to tell. I tell these almost every time: 'The Story-teller,' 'The Five Cabbages,' and 'The Lion on the Path.' Also, there is a ballad called 'The Arkansas Traveler' that uses a dancing man. A dancing man is a wooden jointed 'person.' It makes a noise on wood that sounds like tap dancing."

Robert McKnight, one of the sixth-grade tellers in the April 1993 DODDS Storytelling Festival, said, "I looked through a lot of folktale books, but I didn't like any of the stories until I found 'The Riddle of

Freedom' [in Virginia Hamilton's *The People Could Fly*]." Not all stories are found in books. Scott Fugal, another sixth-grade teller in that festival, chose to tell a hilarious tale he heard from his Danish-American grand-father.

Sometimes you might like to select a story to fit the special place where you will be telling. When Lori Prince told a story at a DODDS festival, it took place in Hanau, home of the Grimm Brothers. She wanted to tell a story from their famous collection of folktales. But she selected "The Seven Swabians," because it is not as well known as some of the other tales.

Perhaps the best advice for those of you who wish to become young tellers is to trust the judgment of the adult who is working with you, especially if that adult has had a lot of storytelling practice. That person will probably be able to steer you to good stories with which to make your start as a storyteller.

If you are working pretty much on your own, then try to listen to tellers who have many years of experience. Or look for printed collections of stories compiled by such tellers. You can find the titles of some collections in the bibliography. If your school or public library has a copy of *Stories: A List of Stories to Tell and Read Aloud,* that will also help you.

Some things to look for in the first stories you tell

Even if you feel you have the best storyteller in the world as your model and teacher, you have to find a story for your style. These are some guidelines that almost all the experts seem to agree on:

1. You have to like the story.
2. It should be short. Beginners in anything, whether it's sports or

music or storytelling, should start with short segments and build up.

3. It helps if the story comes from your own culture, or a similar one.
4. It is easier to start with a story that has a fair amount of repetition.
5. The story should have at least one memorable moment, or a surprise twist, or a deeply satisfying ending.

One or more of these qualities was mentioned by *all* the young storytellers to whom I have spoken or who have written to me, or whose comments were passed on by a teacher.

Learning the story

I believe that storytelling cannot really be taught. It can be demonstrated. The demonstrator/storyteller can point out specific techniques that might not have been obvious to the listeners/learners. But the actual learning of the story can only be done by you, through practice, practice, practice.

There are different ways of learning, and it does help to recognize which way you seem to learn best. The following questions might help you to decide the way to approach learning your first stories.

Are you an imitator?

Some artists feel they must spend hours in front of famous paintings, learning how to paint just like the great artists did. Athletes will often imitate the precise physical movements of a famous person in their sport, hoping that by doing so they will improve their own ability.

If imitating has helped you in some other area of your life, then you may want to try it with storytelling. Find a storyteller you really like, and ask that person if he or she has a tape, preferably a videotape, of a favorite short story. Or use a commercially produced tape. Your local library probably has a number of them. Play the tape over and over, listening for all the pauses, special emphases on certain words, and any voice changes. Try to tell the story in exactly the same way, along with the tape. Gradually reduce the sound and keep telling the story in that same way, but trying not to listen to the original teller's voice. After a dozen or so repetitions you will probably be able to tell it in almost the same way as that teller.

Then tell the story in that same way to as many persons or groups as you can find willing to listen to you. It is important at this stage not to tell it to yourself, but to at least one other person each time. After the first few times you will probably notice that you have begun to change small things in the story. Perhaps you use one or two words that are different, or you are making shorter or longer pauses. You are still basically imitating the original teller, but you have begun to put your own personal stamp on the story.

If you tell your story in public, be sure to give credit to the teller you learned from by imitation.

Are you a memorizer?

When I was in grade school many years ago, we had to memorize a poem every week. Most of my classmates would groan and moan about this assignment, especially if the poem was a long one. I never said so aloud, but I loved such assignments. For me, memorizing was very easy. When I became a children's librarian in the New York Public Library, I found out that my memorizing skills were very useful. We were supposed to tell stories just the way they were printed in books. So most of the first stories I told professionally I learned by memorizing.

Some schools still insist that the students memorize poems and stories. If the story you are supposed to memorize has already been recorded by a professional teller, you can listen to it and memorize the telling, instead of just the words. If it is not on a tape, then make your own recording. Record your telling after you know the story pretty well and can tell most of it without having to look down at a printed version.

Each time you find that you have added something new, such as a better emphasis or a longer pause, rerecord yourself. Keep telling it with the sound of your recorded voice in the background until you are quite confident you know it well. Then gradually lower the sound of the tape, as mentioned above. Start to tell the story to others only when you feel you can do it without having to stop and listen to the tape.

If you memorize better by reading paragraphs over and over again in a printed version of the story, do it that way. Just be sure that you keep the whole story in mind. You don't want to come to the end of a paragraph, only to find you can't remember what words start the next one.

Are you a spur-of-the-moment improvisor?

Do you like telling short jokes and funny stories? Are you the type who comes home after school and tells your family all the things that happened in your day, sometimes in such great detail that they have to ask you to stop? Then you should choose to tell stories that can be put in your own words. Many folktales are of this type. This does not mean that you can successfully tell such stories entirely in your own words. In most cases it will be necessary to keep a few key words of the story as you first heard or read it.

For example, let us say you decide to tell the story "The Three Little Pigs" in your own words, making it a funny, modern story with a new twist. Because the story is so well known, the audience will be expecting to hear, "I'll huff and I'll puff and I'll blow your house down." You might choose, as Sarah Burman of Minneapolis did, to make it the story of "The Three Little Wolves and the Big Bad Pig." In that case it will be the Big Bad Pig who says those fierce, threatening words. You would lose some of the effect of the story if you left out that familiar threat.

If you are an improvisor, make sure that the words you choose to tell your story sound "right" to you *and* to your audience. Katherine Wittenberg, a young teller at the St. Louis Storytelling Festival, said that "the hardest part about perfecting my storytelling was to pick out the right words for what story I was telling." Although she likes improvising, she recognizes that she sometimes needs the guidance of her story-telling teacher, Ruthilde Kronberg, to point out where the words do not really fit the story.

Are you a picturer?

Do you learn best of all by seeing something pictured or put in a diagram? Do you like to write down notes? Then you might like to try drawing a storyboard. A storyboard is a series of rough picture sketches used by many filmmakers to plan the way in which they will film a certain story sequence. Each picture shows a key moment in the story. Quite a number of storytellers, young and old, use this technique to learn a story. One of the student storytellers in the Troupe of Tellers from Eugene, Oregon, likes to choose the stories she tells by going to the library and searching for picture book folktales. She is using the storyboard technique, but in her case the pictures were drawn by professional illustrators.

Ruth Johnson, a teacher in Sprucecourt School in Toronto, recommends picture books from other countries, with easy-to-tell stories, for her students to begin their storytelling practice. The student tellers are forced to remember the words of the story, because they cannot read the words of the original picture book, but they do have the pictures to help them along. The middle grade children especially enjoy using a series of cloth books from Brazil to practice their telling on the youngest classes in the school. Ve, whose family is originally from Vietnam, says, "When I tell a cloth book story, the children are very quiet, and I like that. I like it when the children want me to tell it again. So storytelling is good because it helps me to be a friend to all the children in this school."

Raven, whose family is of Cambodian heritage, is quite sure that telling the stories "helps me to talk good English. I feel good telling the stories like this."

Here is a storyboard of "The Orphan Boy" from this collection (see page 63). Perhaps it can help you learn how to make your own storyboards, if that is a technique that will help you. If you wish to try using picture books in other languages, ask at your local public library if they can get some for you on special loan.

Performing the stories

Once you have learned a story pretty well, you will probably want to perform it in public. There are a few storytellers who tell only to their families and close friends, but most want to share their tales with an audience that includes persons they don't know, or at least don't know well.

Performing a story is not the same as telling it to yourself or a family member or close friend. Performance implies communicating or showing something under slightly more formal or controlled conditions. Even telling while you are baby-sitting can be a performance, if you ask the child or children to sit in a special place facing you as you tell the story, and you invite them to respond to your story. You might do this in words, or gestures, or just by using a special tone of voice or a pause at a key

30

point. Margaret Read MacDonald, in *The Storyteller's Start-up Book,* likes to call this "playing the story."

Again, try not to confuse storytelling with theater. Unless you are doing group stories that are part storytelling, part theater, don't think of the place you will sit or stand as a stage. The place I least like to tell stories from is a stage in front of a big auditorium. I know other storytellers who feel the same way.

The spot you select for telling stories should be one that helps you and your audience feel you are close to each other, part of one group. For most of the time, you as the teller will be the leader of the group, but you must be open to the moments when the audience, by its reactions, expands on the story or leads you in a slightly different direction.

For example, when I first began to tell "The Bear and the Seven Little Children" (see page 55), I used nesting dolls, but I would line them up on a table at my side. After a few times of telling it like that, I told it to a family audience. A little girl was sitting very close to me. When she heard me say, "went to hide under the table," the little girl picked up the doll from the top of the table and put it under the table. When I said, "went to hide under the chair," she hid the next doll under the chair. I quickly realized that it was important for little children in the audience to see the dolls actually being moved off to different spots as though they were hiding. So from then on I changed my way of telling the story.

Josh Williams, one of the Conneaut Traveling Storytellers, liked being close enough to the audience so that he could see the faces of the children. He found that the most enjoyable part of storytelling was not only being able to hear the laughter but also to watch the smiles and grins.

Some of you may like to have the audience seated in a circle for story listening, but I find it hard to keep eye contact with everyone in a circle. For me, the semicircle is ideal. Often, however, the teller is given no choice. The performance must take place in this auditorium or that class-room or this multipurpose room or that lunchroom. Sometimes it must take place on a paved or grassy spot outdoors. It is a good idea if you can visit the storytelling spot before you are scheduled to tell stories. If you cannot, at least try to get a good description of it.

Opening lines

If the audience has not been told much about you or your storytelling, give a sentence or two of introduction. For instance, you might say something like, "I'm in eighth grade but I have been telling stories ever since fifth grade, when Larry Johnson was my teacher. One of the stories I learned while I was in his class was_____and I'd like to tell it to you now. It is a folktale from_____but I tell it in my own way."

If you are one of many performers in a group program, give your name and the name of your story, but don't repeat that information if it was given by someone who introduced you. Instead, go right into your story. For a festival or contest sponsored by your school or some other agency, follow the directions given in the rules or guidelines. If they ask you to state only your name and the title of your story, do just that. But do it in a storytelling manner. For example: "My name is_____and the story I'd like to tell you is 'The Orphan Boy,' a dilemma tale from West Africa."

Pacing your story

Almost all new storytellers go through their stories at too fast a pace. It is very hard to remember to slow down, and to make pauses at just the right moments. Remember, you know the story very well, but your audience may not know it at all. Emphasize key words and repeat them if you see puzzlement on the faces of some audience members. You can repeat whole sentences, saying the words a bit more slowly the second time. If you are using music or drawings or objects in your story, be sure your timing is practiced until it's perfect.

Facial expressions

"The hardest part was deciding where I wanted to use facial expressions," wrote Johnny, one of the students at Northeast Elementary School in a course taught by Martha Hamilton and Mitch Weiss, known as Beauty and the Beast. Another student of theirs, Peter from Fayetteville Elementary School, wrote pretty much the same thing, and said the reason facial expression was so hard was "because I thought I would feel stupid doing it."

Facial expressions do not have to be exaggerated. But your face does have to tell the same story your lips are telling. Of course, if you are telling a tall tale, the best expression is an earnest or serious deadpan. In such a case part of the fun is to see how successful you can be in *not* laughing at your own story.

Distractions during storytelling

Do whatever you can to prevent distractions in advance. In a school I always ask if there is any way to turn off the intercom to the area in which I will be performing. I don't want a message coming out of the intercom at the precise moment I am in the middle of an exciting story. But always try to be so focused in your stories that even if an interruption should occur, you can handle it with aplomb.

If a child interrupts with a question while you are telling, do not stop to answer unless the answer can be worked into the story in a natural way. For example, let us say you are telling "The Noisy Gecko" (see page 43). Perhaps you have explained, at the beginning, that a gecko is a small lizard, but a little child in the audience was not listening, or has already forgotten, and interrupts to ask, "What's a gecko?" Simply insert in your story a sentence like this: "Now remember, a gecko is a small lizard that likes to eat insects."

Often, it is best to ignore the questions of individual audience members and wait to answer them after the story is finished. Sometimes an interruption can add to the storytelling. One of the student tellers in the DODDS Storytelling Festival came to a place in the story that used the words "that's funny," meaning "that's odd." A child in the audience (the little brother of one of the participants) burst out into a loud belly laugh. This made the audience laugh, even though the story was not funny at that point. But the teller repeated herself and said, "Yes, that *is* funny, isn't it!" and went on with her story as soon as the audience had quieted down again.

What if you forget part of the story?

Whether you have memorized your story or are telling it in your own words, there will come a time when you will probably forget some key point in the story. This happens to all of us. You have probably watched some of the funny television programs that show the "bloopers" that actors or announcers or others have made, either in rehearsals or while they were being filmed for an actual program. The same thing happens in live storytelling.

Don't panic if you realize you've left out a key point. Think about your story. Usually there is a way that a forgotten portion of the story can be worked in. Again using the example of the story "The Bear and the Seven Little Children," I can recall that in one of my early tellings I forgot to have Granny mention the Bear before she went off to buy oil. After all but the littlest child had locked the doors and windows and hidden, I said the "Thump, Thump, Thump!" but then added a sentence, as though it were spoken by the oldest girl: "Oh, that must be that big brown Bear who's been sniffing around our house of late; hurry and hide, Mashele!" The story was less suspenseful, but at least it made sense, and I doubt if the children in the audience noticed that I hesitated slightly at that spot.

One of the fourth graders in a class taught by Mitch Weiss and Martha Hamilton was also surprised at how the audience overlooked a mistake. That student wrote, "I felt I had done a good job but by mistake I left out some [of the story] but nobody knew!"

If you cannot quickly find a way to work in the left-out part, simply pause and say something like, "Now, I forgot to tell you something important," and go on to fill in what is needed to make the story clear.

When performing in a contest, you might feel a bit more nervous than when you are telling stories in your class at school. Forget about the judges and simply have fun. I have been a judge at a number of such contests, and the young storytellers who have impressed me most were those who were obviously enjoying their stories. I always overlooked a mistake or stumble here or there if I could see that the teller was really into the story, projecting it to me as clearly as pictures on a movie screen.

Ending your story

Many new storytellers, young and old, are so glad to have finished their public performance that they rush the ending and then hurry to sit down or leave the area. Unless your ending is supposed to be fast and furious, as in "Master of All Masters" (page 100), take the time to be extra slow during the final sentences. Use the closing formula that is common to the folktales from the culture that is the source of your story.

Don't be afraid to repeat the last sentence or idea. If you were telling a dilemma story such as "The Orphan Boy" (page 63) in a contest or festival, you would not be allowed to engage the audience in a discussion after the story. But you would want them to be thinking about the way they would end the story. After asking the three questions, with a pause between each, it would be quite appropriate to repeat at the very end, "Who *was* responsible for that boy's success?"

Keeping track of your telling

It is a good idea to make a few notes to yourself after each of your performances. It helps to use an evaluation sheet.

A fourth grader from Ithaca, New York, who used an evaluation sheet after telling a story wrote, "I felt that I had done something brave because it's hard to tell a story in front of a crowd of people." Another fourth-grade student wrote that her feelings toward the audience changed a lot after her first public performance "because they pay attention and in the end they clap . . . so I wasn't scared anymore."

Here is a sample evaluation sheet. Add other questions if you find them useful in helping to improve your storytelling.

Place where storytelling session was held _____
Type of audience (give number & age range) _____
   (For example, 25 first graders & teacher, ages 6 and about 35)
Story or stories told _____

Did the story or stories appeal to the audience? _____

At which point(s) did audience laugh? _____

_____

At which point(s) did audience react in other ways?_____

_____

Did some in audience get distracted or lose interest? _____

If yes, what was the reason? _____

_____

Use of voice—Was it loud enough? _____

    Did it use several tones rather than a monotone? _____

    Was the pronunciation clear? _____

    Was the pace too fast or too slow? _____

Use of body—Was there eye contact with audience? _____

    Were there too many or too few gestures? _____

    Did it feel natural to stand or to sit? _____

What was the best part of this storytelling session? _____

_____

What parts could have been better? _____

Name _____ Date _____

Start telling!

Whether you are doing it for a school assignment or for your baby-sitting job, for a public performance in front of a big festival audience or a small one in your Sunday school class, for your friends at camp or during a sleep-over, start your storytelling. You will never know if you have a talent for it unless you try it.

The next part of this book has a selection of stories that can get you started.

Part Three

STORIES FOR YOUNG PEOPLE TO TELL

The stories given here all have some unusual twist to them. They are divided into various categories. Many of them could fit into two or three of the categories. I selected these story types because they were the ones most frequently mentioned by the young tellers I talked to or corresponded with while writing this book. There are many other types of stories that appeal to young tellers and listeners.

If you need a story to fit a specific category that is not mentioned here, the best place to go for advice is to the storytellers in your area. There are now many storytelling groups that meet regularly, and the members would probably welcome your interest. There are even some that welcome junior members. You can find out about such groups by contacting the National Story League, c/o Marian Kiligas, 259 East 41 Street, Norfolk, Virginia 23504. Or look in the *National Storytelling Directory,* which is published annually by the National Storytelling Association, P.O. Box 309, Jonesborough, Tennessee 37659.

Another good option is to go to the largest children's library in your area. Chances are they will have a reference collection of storytelling materials. Often, the children's librarian will be a member of the local storytelling group or at least will know if there is one.

Cumulative tales

Cumulative stories are found in almost all parts of the world. They are often called formula tales because they usually have a very strict logic and the basic chant or refrain should not be changed. When telling stories that build up to an ever-longer series of episodes or actions, imagine that you are adding both instruments and faster tempo to a piece being played by an orchestra. This will help to achieve the effect of a crescendo.

Little children like to see each thing pictured. If you decide to use felt figures with these tales, be sure each one is cut out in a recognizable, pleasing outline. Perhaps the making of such sets of figures can be a part of an art class project. For the background, purchase a half yard of good quality felt from a fabric store. Select a pale blue or light green. Use masking tape across the top to attach the background felt to any large surface such as a flip chart easel or slanted blackboard, or even a flat wall. The figures will cling nicely to the surface of the large felt piece if you press each one in place.

The Noisy Gecko
Indonesia

This tale is found throughout the South Pacific. The
Filipino version ("The Trial
of the Animals") is a "why
mosquitos buzz in ears"
story. Try to repeat the animal sounds the way they are
written here, because that is
how they are generally spoken in Bahasa, the language
of Indonesia.

One night, in a village in Indonesia, the village chief was awakened by
the sound of "tok-keh, tok-keh, tok-keh!" **(Pronounce this with intonation up—"tok"—then slight pause, then intonation down—
"keh.")** It was Gecko, the lizard, complaining to the chief.

When the chief asked Gecko what he was complaining about, Gecko
replied, "Firefly keeps shining in my eyes and I cannot sleep."

The chief went to Firefly and asked him why he was shining in
Gecko's eyes. "I heard Woodpecker drumming," replied Firefly. "All day
and all evening he has been going 'tuk, tuk, tuk, trrrrrrrrrrrrrr' so I
thought it was a message calling everyone to a meeting. I was flashing
my light to pass on the message."

The chief went to Woodpecker. "Why are you drumming 'tuk, tuk, tuk,
trrrrrrrrrrrrrr?' Firefly thinks you are sending a message so he keeps
flashing his light in Gecko's eyes. Gecko cannot sleep and now he has

43

awakened everyone with his 'tok-keh, tok-keh, tok-keh.' We want to go back to sleep."

"I was sending a message," said Woodpecker. "I heard Frog go 'kung, kung, kung, kung' all evening and I was sure it was a warning about an earthquake coming so I decided to pass it on."

The chief went to Frog. "Why have you been calling out 'kung, kung, kung, kung' all evening? Woodpecker thinks it is a warning of an earthquake. He keeps drumming 'tuk, tuk, tuk, trrrrrrrrrrrrrr.' Firefly thinks that is a message calling everyone to a meeting so he keeps flashing his light in Gecko's eyes. Gecko cannot sleep and now he has awakened everyone with his 'tok-keh, tok-keh, tok-keh.' We want to go back to sleep."

"I was protesting," said Frog. "I saw Beetle walking down the road carrying some dung and I thought he should not dirty up our road."

The chief went to Beetle. "Why are you carrying dung while walking right down the middle of the road? Frog protests with his 'kung, kung, kung, kung' that it makes the road dirty. Woodpecker thinks Frog is sending a warning about an earthquake so he sends the message on with his 'tuk, tuk, tuk, trrrrrrrrrrrrrr.' Firefly hears Woodpecker and thinks it is a message calling everyone to a meeting. He keeps flashing his light in Gecko's eyes. Gecko cannot sleep and now he has awakened everyone with his 'tok-keh, tok-keh, tok-keh.' We want to go back to sleep."

"I was only cleaning up after Water Buffalo," said Beetle. "He dropped his dung right in the middle of the road and I thought it was my duty to clean it up."

The chief went to Water Buffalo. "Why do you drop your dung in the middle of the road? Beetle thinks it is his duty to clean it up. Frog sees Beetle and protests with his 'kung, kung, kung, kung.' Woodpecker thinks Frog is sending a warning about an earthquake so he passes it on with his 'tuk, tuk, tuk, trrrrrrrrrrrrrr.' Firefly hears Woodpecker and thinks he is calling everyone to a meeting. Firefly keeps flashing his light in Gecko's eyes and Gecko cannot sleep. Now he has awakened everyone with his 'tok-keh, tok-keh, tok-keh.' We want to go back to sleep."

"I was only trying to make the road even," said Water Buffalo. "Rain washes away the stones and makes big holes in the road and I felt I could fill them up."

The chief went to Rain. "Rain, why do you wash away the stones and make big holes in the road? Water Buffalo fills them with his dung. Beetle thinks it is his duty to clean it up. Frog sees Beetle and protests with his 'kung, kung, kung, kung.' Woodpecker thinks Frog is sending a warning about an earthquake so he passes it on with his 'tuk, tuk, tuk, trrrrrrrrrrrrrr.' Firefly hears Woodpecker and thinks it is a message calling everyone together. He keeps flashing his light in Gecko's eyes and Gecko cannot sleep. Now Gecko has awakened everyone with his 'tok-keh, tok-keh, tok-keh.' We want to go back to sleep."

"I don't understand," said Rain. "If I don't come and fill some holes with water, there are no mosquitos, and without mosquitoes, Gecko would go hungry. So tell him to stop his complaining."

The chief went back to Gecko. "We all have our place in life, Gecko. The animals are all trying to do what they think is right. If I order them to do something not in keeping with their nature, something even worse might happen than being kept awake. I suggest you go back and try to hide in a corner where Firefly's flashing cannot reach you. Then we can all get some sleep."

The Little Girl and Her Oninga
Namibia

This is a never-ending story. It was often used at bedtime, and
the teller would continue until all children were asleep. Tell it
while baby-sitting and see how long the children stay awake.
An oninga is a fruit similar to the plum.

A little girl was walking under a tree and all of a sudden a large, ripe
oninga fell from the tree right into her hands. She decided to share it
with her friends. As she walked past her mother, the girl said, "Mother,
why do you not say, 'My firstborn, give me the oninga'? Do you think I
would refuse to share it?"

So the mother said, "My firstborn, give me the oninga." After giving
her mother the fruit, the girl went off to look for her friends. Her mother ate the fruit. After some time, the girl came back and said, "Mother,
where is my oninga?"

"Which oninga?"

"The one that fell from the tree into my hands and that I gave to you."
But the mother had eaten the whole fruit, so to appease her daughter
she gave her a needle. The girl walked on and came upon her father,
sewing new thong sandals for himself. But he had no needle so he was
sewing them with a long thorn.

"Father, why do you sew with a thorn? Why do you not say, 'My firstborn, lend me your needle'?"

So her father said, "My firstborn, lend me your needle." The girl gave
him the needle and walked away to look for her friends. Her father
sewed his thongs with the needle but then he broke it.

When his daughter returned she asked, "Where is my needle?"

"Which needle?"

"The one my mother gave me in place of the oninga."

"Which oninga?"

"The oninga that fell from the tree right into my hands."

But the father had broken the needle so to appease his daughter he gave her an axe. She walked on a bit further and came upon her uncle throwing big stones at a tree branch. He was trying to get at the honey inside. She said to her uncle, "Why don't you say, 'Firstborn of my sister, lend me your axe'?"

Her uncle said, "Firstborn of my sister, lend me your axe."

The girl gave it to him and walked off, still in search of her friends. Her uncle chopped down the tree, but in doing so he broke the axe. However, he had found a huge mound of honey. When the girl returned she asked, "Where is my axe?"

"Which axe?"

"The one my father gave me in place of the needle."

"Which needle?"

"The one my mother gave me in place of the oninga."

"Which oninga?"

"The one that fell from the tree into my hands."

But the uncle had broken the axe so to appease the girl he gave her a pot full of honey. The girl walked along further until she came to her grandmother's house. She saw her grandmother eating a dish of porridge but it had no flavor. So she said, "Grandmother, why don't you say, 'Firstborn of my firstborn, give me some honey'?"

"Firstborn of my firstborn, why don't you give me some honey?" repeated her grandmother. The girl gave her some honey, and the grandmother immediately put some on her porridge. While the girl wandered off to look for her friends, the grandmother used the rest of the honey to make sweet cakes. Soon the girl returned.

"Where is my honey?"

"Which honey?"

"The honey my uncle gave me in place of the axe."

"Which axe?"

"The axe my father gave me in place of the needle."

"Which needle?"

"The needle my mother gave me in place of the oninga."

"Which oninga?"

"The oninga that fell from the tree into my hands."

But her grandmother had used up all the honey so to appease her granddaughter she gave her a basket full of the sweet cakes. The girl walked on a bit further and she came upon a flock of chickens scratching in the dust. They were trying to find something to eat. The girl called out to them, "Chickens, why don't you say, 'Little girl, crumble some of your sweet cakes for us'?" So the chickens did just that and the girl crumbled a few of the sweet cakes until they were crumbs and scattered them on the ground. The rest of the cakes she left in the basket at the side of the road and went off for a while to look for

her friends. The chickens were not satisfied with the crumbs she had given them. They pulled at the cakes in the basket and soon they had eaten them all.

When the girl returned she asked, "Where are my sweet cakes?"

"Which sweet cakes?"

"The ones my grandmother gave me in place of the honey."

"Which honey?"

"The honey my uncle gave me in place of the axe."

"Which axe?"

"The axe my father gave me in place of the needle."

"Which needle?"

"The needle my mother gave me in place of the oninga."

"Which oninga?"

"The oninga that dropped from the tree into my hands."

But the chickens had eaten all the sweet cakes so to appease the girl they each plucked some downy feathers from their breasts and gave them to the girl. She put them in a sack and walked along further until she came upon her cousin minding a flock of sheep and a few cows. Her cousin was plucking loose hairs from the sheep and when the girl asked him why he was doing that, he said he wanted to make a pillow.

"Why don't you say, 'Firstborn of my father's sister, lend me some feathers'?" the girl asked her cousin.

So her cousin said, "Firstborn of my father's sister, lend me some feathers." The girl handed him the bag of feathers and told him to be careful when taking some feathers out. She went off to look for her friends and while she was gone her cousin opened the sack. But he was careless and opened it too wide. A puff of wind came along and blew all of the feathers away.

When the girl returned she asked, "Where are my feathers?"

"Which feathers?"

"The ones the chickens gave me in place of the sweet cakes."

"Which sweet cakes?"

"The ones my grandmother gave me in place of the honey."

"Which honey?"

"The honey my uncle gave me in place of the axe."

"Which axe?"

"The axe my father gave me in place of the needle."

"Which needle?"

"The needle my mother gave me in place of the oninga."

"Which oninga?"

"The oninga that fell from the tree right into my hands." But the feathers were gone so her cousin milked one of the cows and gave her a gourd full of milk. The girl walked along until she came upon a cat. It meowed pitifully, it was so hungry.

The girl said, "Cat, why don't you say, 'Little girl, give me some of the milk in the gourd'?" The cat only meowed, but the girl took pity on him and poured out some of the milk for him to drink. She left the gourd there and went in search of her friends. The cat tipped the gourd over and lapped up all the rest of the milk. When the girl returned she asked the cat, "Where is my milk?"

But the cat did not answer. It ran away and climbed a tree and left the girl standing there.

NOTE: I have given this an arbitrary ending with the cat. End the story earlier if you wish, or continue it by having the cat give something to the girl.

Little Chick with the Dirty Beak
Latin America

Here is another cumulative tale with much repetition. This story can be found in the folklore of most Spanish-speaking peoples. Again, if you wish to have an easier time remembering who comes next in the story, make felt figures. Try to say the last part, between the dashes, in one breath.

Little Chick was all dressed up. She was on her way to the wedding of her uncle Parrot when she saw a grain of wheat in the muddy path. "Shall I pick it up or not?" she asked herself. "If I don't pick it I'll lose the grain. If I pick it up I'll make my beak dirty and I can't go with a dirty beak to the wedding of my Uncle. Pick it or not pick it—what shall I do?"

Well, she picked it up and she made her beak dirty. She went to Grass and said, "Grass, clean my beak so I can go to the wedding of my uncle Parrot."

But the Grass said, "I don't want to."

Little Chick went walking along, walking along, until she met Goat. "Goat, eat Grass. Grass won't clean my beak and I can't go to the wedding of my uncle Parrot."

But the Goat said, "I don't want to."

Little Chick went walking along, walking along, until she met Stick. "Stick, beat Goat. Goat won't eat

Grass, Grass won't clean my beak, and I can't go to the wedding of my uncle Parrot."

But Stick said, "I don't want to."

Little Chick went walking along, walking along, until she met Fire. "Fire, burn Stick. Stick won't beat Goat, Goat won't eat Grass, Grass won't clean my beak, and I can't go to the wedding of my uncle Parrot."

But Fire said, "I don't want to."

Little Chick went walking along, walking along, until she met Water. "Water, quench Fire. Fire won't burn Stick, Stick won't beat Goat, Goat won't eat Grass, Grass won't clean my beak, and I can't go to the wedding of my uncle Parrot."

But Water said, "I don't want to."

Little Chick went walking along, walking along, until she met Burro. "Burro, drink Water. Water won't quench Fire, Fire won't burn Stick, Stick won't beat Goat, Goat won't eat Grass, Grass won't clean my beak, and I can't go to the wedding of my uncle Parrot."

But the Burro said, "I don't want to."

Little Chick went walking along, walking along, until she met Horsefly. "Horsefly, sting Burro. Burro won't drink Water, Water won't quench Fire, Fire won't burn Stick, Stick won't beat Goat, Goat won't eat Grass, Grass won't clean my beak, and I can't go to the wedding of my uncle Parrot."

But Horsefly said, "I don't want to."

Little Chick went walking along, walking along, until she met Dog. "Dog, snap at Horsefly. Horsefly won't sting Burro, Burro won't drink Water, Water won't quench Fire, Fire won't burn Stick, Stick won't beat Goat, Goat won't eat Grass, Grass won't clean my beak, and I can't go to the wedding of my uncle Parrot."

But Dog said, "I don't want to."

Little Chick went walking along, walking along, until she met Rope. "Rope, tie up Dog. Dog won't snap at Horsefly, Horsefly won't sting Burro, Burro won't drink Water, Water won't quench Fire, Fire won't burn Stick, Stick won't beat Goat, Goat won't eat Grass, Grass won't clean my beak, and I can't go to the wedding of my Uncle Parrot."

But Rope said, "I don't want to."

Little Chick went walking along, walking along, until she met Rat. "Rat, chew Rope. Rope won't tie up Dog, Dog won't snap at Horsefly, Horsefly won't sting Burro, Burro won't drink Water, Water won't quench Fire, Fire won't burn Stick, Stick won't beat Goat, Goat won't eat Grass, Grass won't clean my beak, and I can't go to the wedding of my Uncle Parrot."

But the Rat said, "I don't want to."

Little Chick went walking along, walking along, until she met Cat. "Cat, chase Rat. Rat won't chew Rope, Rope won't tie up Dog, Dog won't snap at Horsefly, Horsefly won't sting Burro, Burro won't drink Water, Water won't quench Fire, Fire won't burn Stick, Stick won't beat Goat, Goat won't eat Grass, Grass won't clean my beak, and I can't go to the wedding of my Uncle Parrot."

And Cat said, "If you will give me a saucer of milk, I will do what you ask." So Little Chick ran to get a saucer of milk. She put it in front of Cat. Cat lapped it up and then—Cat began to chase Rat, Rat began to chew on Rope, Rope began to tie up Dog, Dog began to snap at Horsefly, Horsefly began to sting Burro, Burro began to drink Water, Water began to quench Fire, Fire began to burn Stick, Stick began to beat Goat, Goat began to eat Grass, Grass cleaned off Little Chick's beak, and—she was able to go to the wedding of her Uncle Parrot.

Stories that use dramatic devices
or objects in the telling

Different peoples have used dramatic devices in storytelling for thousands of years. Sometimes these devices were limited to a clever and unusual use of the body, or of the voice, or of a musical instrument. In other cases it was verbal devices, such as abrupt or open endings, that caused the audience to pay extra attention. In still other situations the teller used picture drawing, or objects, to make things in the story seem more concrete.

One of the most interesting uses of objects in storytelling was the story vine or net often carried by West African traveling tellers. On the net or vine would be hung objects made of bone, straw, metal, or shell. Each object represented a story in the teller's repertoire. The net or vine was hung in an area where numerous people were likely to pass by, such as a marketplace. The teller hoped someone would be intrigued enough by an object to ask for that story. Of course, the teller expected payment before beginning the story!

The Bear and the Seven Little Children
Poland

This story is easily recognizable as a different version of "The Wolf and the Seven Little Kids." I recommend the use of a set of seven or eight nesting dolls to tell this story. If you can find only a set that includes six dolls, change the title. If there are eight, let the largest be the grandmother. If there are six or seven, let them represent only the children. Use the name Mashele if the littlest doll represents a girl, Heshele if it represents a boy. Before telling the story, check out the space in front of the audience where you will be standing. Arrange a chair and small table in that space. On the table put a cloth bag. Find corners or ledges that can represent the cupboard, the stove, the bed, and the closet. If you carefully repeat the same phrases each time, you will find the audience participates in the telling by naming the hiding place or joining in on the bear's threat. Should you be telling the story during the holiday season, you might wish to add phrases and action related to Hanukkah. At the opening, after the first paragraph, change the second paragraph and tell it like this:

Now Hanukkah was going to start that evening, and suddenly Granny noticed she had no more oil. "I cannot make latkes, potato pancakes, without oil. And we must have latkes for our first night of Hanukkah. I will have to go to the village to get some." So Granny said to the children, "Children, children . . ."

In the last paragraph, after "safe and sound," add the following:

And that night Granny made a big platter of delicious latkes. After they had lit the first candle and said their special Hanukkah prayers, they sat down to eat. And you know who ate the most pancakes—little Mashele (Heshele)!

There was once a granny who took care of many children. She watched out for them while their mothers and fathers worked. Once in a while Granny had to leave the children alone in the house while she ran to the village to buy goods at the market. Then she would say, "Children, lock all the doors and windows and don't let anyone in except me, your Granny."

Now, one day Granny noticed she had no more oil for cooking. "I must go to the village and get some," she said. "Children, children, lock all the doors and windows and then hide and don't let anyone in, especially not big brown Bear who's been sniffing around our house of late."

Granny went off **(move largest doll off to the side, if you have eight)** and the oldest girl locked the front door after her. Then she went to hide under the table **(place doll under table)**. The next girl came out and locked the side door and she went to hide under the chair **(place next size doll under chair)**. The next girl came out and locked the back door and she went to hide behind the stove **(place next size doll in selected spot)**. The next girl came out and locked the front window and she went to hide under the bed **(place next size doll in selected spot)**. The next girl came out and locked the side window and she went to hide on top of the cupboard **(place next size doll in selected spot)**. The next girl came out and locked the last window, the one in the back, and she went to hide inside the closet **(place next size doll in selected spot)**. Last of all came little Mashele **(Heshele)**. There was nothing left to lock up. There was no place left to hide.

All of a sudden there was a Thump, Thump, Thump. It was the sound of big brown Bear coming close to the house. Quick as a wink Mashele **(Heshele)** jumped inside a bag sitting on the table.

Bear pounded on the door and called out in a gruff voice, "Children, children, open the door. I have sweet berries for you."

The oldest girl, hiding under the table, called back to him, "We know it's you, Bear. We won't open the door for you. We only open it to Granny, with her sweet voice."

So Bear went back to his den and ate some sweet, sweet honey. Then he went back to the house and knocked on the door gently, like Granny would knock, and he said in a honey-soft voice, "Children, children, open the door. I have something nice for you." The oldest girl came out from where she was hiding and—opened—the—door.

In walked great—big—Bear. The oldest girl ran and hid again under the table, but the bear sniffed her out and found her. He picked her up in his big paws and said, "I'm going to take you home and fatten you up and eat you" **(pick up doll under table)**. He sniffed and sniffed and found the one hiding under—the chair **(pick up doll under chair)**. He picked her up in his big paws and said, "I'm going to take you home and fatten you up and eat you." He sniffed and sniffed and found the one hiding behind—the stove **(pick up doll from behind imaginary stove)**. He picked her up in his paws and said, "I'm going to take you home and fatten you up and eat you." He sniffed and sniffed and found the one hiding under—the bed **(pick up doll from under imaginary bed)**. He picked her up in his big paws and said, "I'm going to take you home and fatten you up and eat you." He sniffed and sniffed and found the one hiding on top of—the cupboard **(pick up doll from imaginary cupboard)**. He picked her up in his great big paws and said, "I'm going to take you home and fatten you up and eat you." He sniffed and sniffed and found the one hiding inside—the closet **(pick up doll from imaginary closet)**. He picked her up in his big paws and said, "I'm going to take you home and fatten you up and eat you." And Bear lumbered off to his den with all those children.

Just then Granny came home and she saw the door was open. She called out, "Children, children, where are you?" No answer. She went into the house and called again, "Children, children, where are you?" Then she heard a faint "Here I am." It came from the bag on the table. Out of the bag came Mashele **(Heshele)**.

"Oh, Granny," she said. "Bear came along and he had such a soft voice we thought it was you so the oldest girl opened the door and he took them all and said he was going to fatten them up and eat them."

"Well, never you mind, I know how to take care of bears, I do, I do," said Granny. "You lock the door and go back to your hiding place, and I'll bring back all the children, see if I won't."

Granny took a jar of sweet, sweet honey. She took a jar of cool, cool milk. And last of all, she took a long—white—feather! She went off to the place where Bear had his den and called out, "Barele, Barele, I have some sweet honey for you."

"Hmm, hmm," growled Bear. "I have my own honey."

"Barele, Barele, I have some cool milk for you."

"Hmm, hmm, I don't need milk. Soon I will have little children to eat."

"Barele, Barele, I have a feather—to tickle your ears." Now you may not know it, but bears like nothing better than to have their ears tickled. Have you ever seen bears in a circus? They were trained by having their ears tickled. It's the truth!

Well, when Bear heard that, he said, "Oh, yes, come in and tickle my ears." Granny went in and tickled first one ear and then the other. She tickled and tickled until soon Bear was rolling on the ground, he was

laughing so hard. But Granny just kept on tickling and tickling and pretty soon, Bear laughed so hard, he exploded with laughter!

Granny gathered up the children and she hurried back home with them. "You see," she said to little Mashele **(Heshele)**. "I told you I would bring them back safe and sound." And after that, you may be sure the children never opened the door to anyone but Granny **(line up all dolls in size order on the table).**

The Glutton

Japan

This is one of the many traditional drawing stories passed down orally by Japanese children. They are called *ekaki uta* in Japanese, which means "drawing songs," because each drawing is accompanied by a chant similar to the jump rope chants or game songs of American children. It is almost impossible to translate them word for word, because they are full of puns involving words and numbers and letters. For example, in the drawing song below, the Japanese word for "chess" is *go,* and that is also the word for the number five. The numbers in the text correspond to the numbers in the drawing, and indicate the order in which the figure is drawn. If you see a girl in the figure rather than a boy, substitute with the words given in parentheses.

Once (1),
there was a boy (girl)
named Two-Three (2,3).
One day he (she) went for (4)
a stroll to find someone to play
a game of chess. He (she) played
five (5), no six games (6). He (she)
had a nose for everything but work (7).
But when it came time to eat, he (she)
ate (8) enough for nine (9) or ten persons (10).

The Fisherman's Surprise
United States

This version is slightly adapted from one told by Melissa McCulloch, a student at Eric Smith School in Ramsey, New Jersey. She learned it from friends, who in turn learned it from friends. It is typical of the "trick" stories that start up and spread like wildfire, entirely by word of mouth. To tell this story, you need a one-dollar bill. If you are telling to large audiences, you might want to make a fake dollar bill about three times as large as a real one.

One day a fisherman decided he would go and catch fish in the lake. He had heard there were big catfish waiting to be caught. So he fished in one corner of the lake **(fold over one corner toward the front of a dollar bill),**

then in another corner
(fold over second corner),

then in another corner
(fold over third corner),

and finally in the last corner **(fold over fourth corner so the dollar bill has points on both ends as shown).**

 Finding nothing, he searched both sides of the lake **(fold in half)**.

Then he searched both ends **(open up and fold in half in the other direction, as indicated)**.

 Finally, he asked his friends to bring their boats **(push up on center fold and bring in the sides by pinching together, as indicated)**.

 They surrounded the catfish **(fold as indicated)**.

The fisherman picked up that catfish but as soon as he did, the fish said, "Let me go! Let me go!" **(manipulate the "mouth" of the fish)**. The fisherman was so surprised he dropped the catfish **(drop dollar bill figure)**. And to this day that huge talking catfish still swims in the lake. There he is! **(Pick up figure and pretend to bite a listener's nose. The fish's mouth will show President Washington's face.)**

The Orphan Boy
Liberia

This tale is from the Kpelle people. It is typical of the type of story called a dilemma tale. Such stories are found in many parts of West and central Africa. In a dilemma tale, there should be several equally good answers to the question posed at the end.

Once an opossum stole some kola nuts from a powerful chief. The opossum then ran away with the nuts until he came upon an orphan boy, sleeping out in the open. The opossum put the kola nuts in and around the boy's hands, and then ran off.

The orphan boy was discovered and taken to the chief.

"He must be executed," said the chief. But an old woman was standing nearby and she took pity on the boy, for she suspected he was an orphan.

"Before you execute him, please let him help me grind my rice," she begged. "I need help, and he deserves one last meal before he dies."

The chief said the boy could help her, but as soon as he had eaten his last meal, he was to be brought back.

The orphan boy went to help the woman, and when they had finished grinding the rice and cooking it, she gave a portion to the boy. He was about to eat it when a cat approached and said, "If you give me some of that rice, I will save your life."

The boy gave the cat some of his rice, and after the cat had eaten it, he gave the boy a dead rat. "What can I do with a dead rat," complained the orphan boy, "when I am about to be killed myself?"

Just then a snake came slithering up. "Give me that dead rat and I will save your life," hissed the snake.

The boy gave the dead rat to the snake and as soon as the snake had swallowed it, he turned to the boy and said, "Here is some powerful medicine, made from my venom. Go back to the chief as you have been ordered, but wait at the side until I have come up to the chief's wife. I will bite her, and as soon as she falls over, step forward and say that you have something to cure her."

The orphan boy did as the snake had told him. As soon as he saw the chief's wife fall over lifeless, he stepped forward and offered to cure her.

"If you succeed," said the chief, "I will reward you handsomely."

The boy brought out the medicine, gave it to the wife, and she got well. The chief no longer wanted to execute the orphan boy. Instead, he gave him many gifts. The orphan boy grew up to be rich.

Now, who was responsible for that boy being a successful man today? Was it the old woman? Was it the cat? Was it the snake?

The Bar of Gold
Europe

In many German versions of this story, it is usually a wishing ring that the farmer and his wife find and never use, because it always seems better to them to hold off on asking for the one wish it will grant. Unbeknownst to them, a thief has stolen the actual wishing ring and substituted an ordinary ring in its place. This version is slightly better known, and may well be a literary rewriting of a folktale. Use a gold-colored brick or an unusual ring to add drama to the story.

Long years ago there lived a poor laborer who never knew what it was to sleep in peace. Whether times were bad or good, he was haunted by fears of the future. This constant worrying caused him to look so thin and tired that people hesitated to give him work. He was steady and frugal, and never wasted his time or money in foolish pleasures. His friends agreed he was very worthy of success and good luck, but it rarely came his way.

One day the poor man sat by the roadside with his head in his hands, weeping and moaning. A kindly doctor from a town nearby stopped to talk to him.

"You seem to have troubles, my good man. What can I do to help you?"

The poor laborer wept as he answered the doctor. "I am feeling ill and wonder what will happen to my wife and children if I really get sick and cannot work. I love them dearly and I don't want them to starve. I work as hard as I can but we never seem to have enough to make ends meet."

"Come, come," said the doctor. "Get up and come with me. I can see that if you do not kill worry, worry will kill you." The doctor took the poor man straight home. He gave him a tonic and then took the man into a special room in his house. Against one wall was a glass case, and in the case was a bar of metal resting on a velvet cloth.

"That bar of gold was handed down to me by my father," said the doctor. "He was once as poor as you are now. But by hard work and careful saving, he managed to buy this bar of gold. He told me to keep it and use it only if absolutely necessary. So I studied and worked hard, and many were the times I wanted to cash in that bar of gold, but something always stopped me. I have managed to earn well for many years and I have enough savings for all my future needs. So I will give you the glass case with the bar of gold. Do not break into it if you possibly can avoid it. Always try to earn enough as you go. But remember that the bar of gold is there for you if you absolutely need it."

The poor man could hardly express his thanks to the doctor, he was so overcome. He took the case with the bar of gold home with him and told his wife of the kind doctor who had given it to him.

"We will only touch it if we are in desperate need," agreed his wife.

They hid the case in their bedroom, and the knowledge that it was there seemed to change the man overnight. He was transformed. He sang and whistled at his work, and handled himself with confidence. Soon he had a steady job at good pay. He and his wife would whisper prayers of thanks each night. Their children grew up strong and healthy, and before long they married and started their own families.

One summer evening the man and his wife sat on their porch, watching their grandchildren at play in their yard. Suddenly, a stranger came walking along the road. He was dressed in rough, ragged clothes, but he spoke in a soft, educated voice, asking for something to eat and a place to spend the night. The old man and his wife invited the stranger in and gave him a meal.

"I am a scientist," said the stranger, "but I have fallen on hard times. Because of a mistake I made, I fear I will never get another job." After he had told his long, sad story, the old man and his wife looked at each other and nodded in agreement. They went to get the case with the bar of gold and handed it to the stranger.

"We want to give this bar of gold to you," they said. "A kindly doctor gave it to us in our hour of need, and now we have no further need for it."

Greatly surprised, the stranger took the bar of gold from the old couple and murmured his thanks. But the moment he held the bar in his hands, he knew by its weight that it was not gold. Still, he did not wish to offend the man and his wife, so he took the bar of metal with him when he set off the next day. As soon as he was out of sight of their home he sat down, took out a piece of rag, and began to polish the bar. As he rubbed away, he suddenly noticed that there was a faint inscription hidden on one side. When he had polished the bar until it shone, he could read the inscription: "It is fear of the future that causes unhappiness. Tread the path of life with courage and you will reach the end of your journey."

The stranger smiled and said to himself, "Well, the old couple have given me a valuable gift after all. I shall forget my fears and make a new start in life." And he set off down the road, taking the bar with him.

The Alligator's Whistle
Cuba

Most of the Africans brought to Cuba as slaves spoke Yoruba
or one of the languages of the Congo Delta region. Many
words from these languages survive in Cuban Spanish.
Sometimes the meaning survives, but in other cases they are
used as nonsense or as magical words. In storytelling, African
Cubans frequently intersperse music in the tales. The opening song was used to open the storytelling sessions.

Alligator once had a whistle on which he could play a very nice tune.
He was very proud of his whistle and played it whenever he lay on the
riverbank, resting in the sun. One day Dog went to the river to bathe and
cool off. He heard Alligator playing his whistle.

68

Pi-to ca-si-ba, Pi-to ca-si-ba nué   Con-go na, con-go na

lu-an-ga

"*Ay, compay,* my good buddy, lend me your whistle," begged Dog. Alligator gave the whistle to Dog. Dog began to play a tune.

"*Compay,* you play well," said Alligator. "Now give me back my whistle."

Dog begged to be allowed to play it a little longer, and Alligator consented. But instead of playing the whistle, Dog put it in his mouth and then took off, running from Alligator as fast as he could. As soon as he got far away from the river, Dog started to play the whistle again.

Fin - di - ca - bón   Fin - di - ca - bón

Pi-to ca-si-ba, Pi-to ca-si-ba nué   Con-go na, con-go na

lu-an-ga

He came to a town and started to play the whistle in the square. "Whose whistle is that?" someone asked.

"Oh, it's not mine," answered Dog. "God sent it to me."

"Where do you come from?" they asked.

"From Diangarangon, a strange place far from here," answered Dog. He continued to play his music, and soon he was getting paid for it. He earned a lot of money.

Then one day he heard that a princess had died, and the king was looking for the best musicians to play along with the mourners at the funeral. Dog rushed off so fast, he lost the whistle.

Ever since then, Dog will come running when he hears you whistle. He thinks you have found his whistle. As for Alligator, don't go too near him, especially with Dog. He is still angry about that whistle.

Fin - di - ca - bón Fin - di - ca - bón

Pi-to ca - si - ba, Pi - to ca - si - ba nué Con - go na, con - go na

lu - an - ga

Note: The words to this song are difficult to translate. They are mostly a mixture of Spanish and Congolese, and suggest singing and dancing connotations. They can be loosely translated to mean: "Forget your worries, forget your cares; my little whistle, my little nut whistle, makes you feel like dancing the Congo way."

Stories that are
enhanced by costume

There is often a temptation to confuse storytelling and stage drama. In most cases the storyteller should not be an actor. In storytelling, the teller usually does not try to act the part of one character as described by an author. Actors are usually directed by a person outside of the action who must bring together a group of characters and the scenes they act in and make it all seem realer than real. Storytellers, on the other hand, must get the audience to see all the characters and the scenes, all the while making it clear that they, too, are "looking at" the whole picture of the story, not acting it out. Storytelling is shared viewing (teller and audience) of a kind of movie of the imagination.

Many school festivals and contests do not allow participants to wear costumes. But occasionally, a costume can be helpful when one is trying to re-create a historical period of storytelling. For example, if you wanted to tell a story in the manner of the ancient bards, for a historical program on Saint Patrick's Day or for a Greek or Roman classics day, it would probably add quite a bit to the performance if you were to dress as a bard. There are many pictures of bards in *The World of Storytelling*.

Use costume with great caution, but don't be afraid to use it when it seems called for.

The King's Diamond Cross
Europe

Barbara Snow, of Eugene, Oregon, steered me to this story, which originally appeared in verse form in *St. Nicholas Magazine.* Before telling it, find a velvet cape or mantle, preferably a black or purple full-length one. Ask family members or buy one at a thrift shop. Then buy twenty-five rhinestone buttons, of the type with a loop on the underside that can be sewn or pinned onto cloth. Sew twenty-two of the twenty-five buttons in a cross pattern on the back of the cape, as indicated in the diagram. Then *pin* the last three in the positions indicated, placing the pins on the inside of the cape, of course.

15_a
14_a
13_a
12_a
11_a
$15_b \quad 14_b \quad 13_b \quad 12_b \quad 11_b \quad 10_a \quad 11_c \quad 12_c \quad 13_c \quad 14_c \quad 15_c$
9_a
8_a
7_a
6_a
5_a
4_a
3_a
2_a
1_a

There was once a king who collected diamonds. But unlike many other kings, he did not keep them hidden away. Oh, no. He wanted to see them every day. So the king had his diamonds sewn onto the back of his royal cape. **(Twirl the cape dramatically around, to show the audience the cross pattern of "diamonds.")**

Now, the king not only wanted to *see* his diamonds every day, he wanted to *count* them every day. And he had his own peculiar way of counting. He always started at the bottom. "One, two,

72

three, four, five, six, seven, eight, nine, ten, eleven, twelve, thirteen, four-teen, fifteen," he would count straight up. "One, two, three, four, five, six, seven, eight, nine, ten, eleven, twelve, thirteen, fourteen, fifteen," he would count up from the bottom and then off to the right side of the cross. "One, two, three, four, five, six, seven, eight, nine, ten, eleven, twelve, thirteen, fourteen, fifteen," he would count up from the bottom and then off to the left side of the cross. (**Slowly count the three ways, putting your finger on each "diamond" as you go from the bottom straight up, up and off to the right, and up and off to the left.**)

Every day he would count his diamonds like that. His court treasurer tried to teach him to count in a different way, but the king insisted he wanted to do it his own way. "I get less confused that way," he said. One day the king noticed a tear in one of the seams on his cape. "I must have this mended," he said. So he called for the court tailor. When the court tailor came in, he found the king counting his diamonds one last time before turning the cape over to be mended.

"One, two, three, four, five, six, seven, eight, nine, ten, eleven, twelve, thirteen, fourteen, fifteen, straight up. One, two, three, four, five, six, seven, eight, nine, ten, eleven, twelve, thirteen, fourteen, fifteen, up and to the right. One, two, three, four, five, six, seven, eight, nine, ten, eleven, twelve, thirteen, fourteen, fifteen, up and to the left." When he had fin-ished, the king gave the cape to the tailor.

The tailor had been astonished at the way in which the king counted his diamonds. He took the cape aside, looked at it closely, and then said to himself, "I think I will play a trick on the king." (**At this point show the scissors, needle, and thread. Turn around and do what is indi-cated in the solution below, while saying the following paragraph. Stretch it out if you need more time.**) The tailor brought out his scis-sors, needle, and thread. He sewed very carefully, with the tiniest stitches he could make. He mended the tear in the seam, but he also did something else. He put two of the diamonds in his pocket!

(Turn back to audience, show the two "diamonds," and put them in your pocket.)

When the tailor handed the cape back to the king, the king looked at it a bit puzzled, and then said, "I must count my diamonds, to be sure they are all there." Once more he counted them in his peculiar way. "One, two, three, four, five, six, seven, eight, nine, ten, eleven, twelve, thirteen, fourteen, fifteen, straight up. One, two, three, four, five, six, seven, eight, nine, ten, eleven, twelve, thirteen, fourteen, fifteen, up and to the right. One, two, three, four, five, six, seven, eight, nine, ten, eleven, twelve, thirteen, fourteen, fifteen, up and to the left. Well, they are all there," said the king with satisfaction.

The tailor laughed to himself. He had taken two of the king's diamonds and the king did not even notice. How did he do it?

(Ask a member of the audience to come up and count in the same way. After several minutes, if no one in the audience has come up with the answer, explain the solution. You might wish to ask the question, "Do you think the tailor gave back the diamonds?" It will stimulate a very lively discussion!)

SOLUTION: Unpin and take off the top button—15A—and place it at the very bottom, keeping the space equal to the spaces between the other buttons in the line. Then unpin and take off the two buttons at the ends of the two sides—15B and 15C in the diagram.

Point of View
Cameroon

Clothing from other countries can be used to emphasize a point in a story. If you wish, have a couple wearing a costume (from any part of the world but preferably from West Africa) stroll by you at the appropriate moment toward the end of the story. Make the description match their costume. You will probably get an extra laugh if one of them is carrying a large, lifelike doll wearing nothing!

Spider and Millipede were friends. They went everywhere together. One day they sat talking together and Millipede said to Spider, "My dear, I must tell you that I think humans are unable to hear."

"What makes you say that?" asked Spider.

"Well, when I walk along," said Millipede, "I can hear my feet churning along like a steamboat on the river. They make a noise like this: Urr, urr, urr, urr. But the humans don't seem to hear it at all. They step all over me."

"My friend, you speak the truth," said Spider. "But let me tell you that I think humans are also blind. If I build a lovely house, with walls stretched out and a veranda to sit on, along comes some human, stumbling about and breaking up my house, tearing it all apart. But does that human say one word? No, not even an 'Oh, I'm so sorry.' I have to run through the grass

75

and search for another place to build. I tell you, humans are not only deaf, they are also blind. They seem to see nothing."

Suddenly, Spider and Millipede saw a family walk by. The wife had a patterned cloth draped around her body, and a kerchief was wound high around her head. The husband wore a long white gown with flowing sleeves and carried an open umbrella. Their little baby, however, was bare naked.

"Look," said Spider to Millipede. "I think humans are stupid as well. They start off quite content to go about as God made them, but they end up wearing things like that."

"Yes," nodded Millipede wisely. "Humans are deaf, blind, and stupid."

The Ant and the Grasshopper
Aesop's fable

In ancient Greece there were two main types of storytellers who performed the classic myths and tales. One was the *aoidos*. That is the term Homer used to describe a performer who told the old stories by composing them anew each time, mostly by rearranging well-known phrases and formulaic expressions in new poetic ways. The *aoidos* usually had a musical instrument, such as a lyre, that was used to help the performer keep to a certain rhythm. It also gave the performer time to compose the next verse in his or her head. The rhapsode, on the other hand, usually performed the same stories but by reciting well-known versions. The rhapsode memorized, rather than composing each time. Most rhapsodes carried a tall stick and recited in very dramatic ways, often pounding the stick or waving it for emphasis. They told stories in a very dramatic style.

The following fable could be performed in a Greek or Latin classics course, or anyplace ancient storytelling styles are to be demonstrated. The teller should wear a costume similar to ancient Greek clothing and carry a knobbed stick similar to the one sketched here. The stick should be as tall as the teller. The telling should be somewhat exaggerated.

'Twas that bleak season of the year
In which no smiles, no charms appear.
Bare were the trees; the rivers froze.
The hilltops all were capped with snows.
Lodging was scarce and food was scant,
When Grasshopper addressed the Ant,
And in a supplicating tone,
Begged: "Do not leave me on my own.
It is, indeed, a bitter task
For those who are unused to ask;
Yet I am forced the truth to say
I have not eaten a morsel today.
But you, with so much plenty blessed,
Know how to pity the distressed.
Give me grain from the stores you hold;
The gods will reward you a hundredfold."
The Ant beheld Grasshopper's plight.
Her heart was sorrowed at the sight.
Yet, still inquisitive to know
How he became reduced so low,
Ant asked: "While I worked hard and fast,
What did you do this summer past?"
"In summertime, dear Ant," said he,
"Ah, those were merry months for me!
I thought of nothing but delight,
I sang and danced, both day and night.
Through yonder meadows you did pass;
You must have heard me in the grass."

"Ah!" cried the Ant, and knit her brow,
"It is enough I hear you now.
And Mr. Hopper, to be plain
You seek my charity in vain.
We workers do not share our due
With worthless vagabonds like you!
I have some corn, but none to spare;
Next summer learn to take more care;
And while you frolic, please remember,
July is followed by December."

Stories for
holidays and celebrations

I find it hardest to locate just the right stories for holiday programs or for special occasions. Audience expectations seem different to me at such times. Most of the young people I interviewed for this book did not have experience in holiday storytelling, other than Christmas and Hanukkah. Some of them mentioned that they had been asked to do stories for special occasions and found it difficult.

If you can't find an appealing story related to the holiday itself, select a story that has characters who reflect the emotional and spiritual qualities of that holiday or event. For example, for Presidents' Day, if you did not find any story you liked about Washington or Lincoln, you might tell a story about wisdom and leadership. For a gift-giving holiday, there are many stories that reveal the true meaning of giving.

Why the Menorah Has Its Distinctive Shape
Jewish

Before telling this story, locate one seven-branched menorah (Jewish candelabrum) and one Hanukkah menorah with holders for eight candles. If you kindle lights at the end, do so from right to left, as in the direction of Hebrew writing.

This story is very appropriate for an ecumenical service in which the symbols of the various winter holidays are explained. If you wish to include a Bible verse with this story, read Psalm 30 (Psalm 29 in some Bibles), "A Song for the Dedication of the Temple," after lighting the menorah.

God told Moses to have the princes of the tribes of Israel bring their gifts to the sanctuary, one each day for twelve days. After they had done that, Aaron, the brother of Moses, was very upset.

"It seems as if my tribe has been excluded from participating in the dedication of the sanctuary," he cried.

So God said to Moses, "Go to Aaron and tell him not to feel slighted. On the contrary, he shall enjoy a greater glory than all the princes of Israel, for he is to light the lamps in the sanctuary."

When the people of Israel heard God's command that lights were to be lit in the sanctuary, they said, "O Lord of the World! You order us to make a light for you, but you are the light of the world."

God replied, "I did not ask you to burn lamps for me because I need light. By your own eyes you can see how little need I have of your light. You have the white of the eye and the dark of the eye, and it is by means of the dark of the eye that you are enabled to see, not through the white of the eye. A human person lights one light by means of another that is already burning, but I have brought forth light out of darkness. I commanded you to light the lamps in the sanctuary so that your souls, which are the lamps of the Lord, may be protected from all evil."

Now at the same time that Moses received the command to light the sanctuary, he also received instructions in how to fashion the menorah. But Moses found it difficult to carry out the instructions, for he did not know how to go about constructing it. It seemed so complicated.

God then said to Moses, "I shall show you a model." God took white fire, red fire, green fire, and black fire, and out of these four kinds of fire he fashioned a menorah.

But Moses, no matter how he tried, was not able to copy it, so he went back to God. At that, God took Moses' hand and drew a design of the menorah on his palm, saying, "Look at this, and when you make the menorah, imitate the design I have drawn here."

But even that did not succeed in teaching Moses, so he returned to God in great distress. God quieted him with these words: "Go to Bezalel. He will do it right." And indeed, Bezalel had no difficulty in making the menorah, for he was the one who had designed the tabernacle. As soon as Moses showed him the design in the palm of his hand, Bezalel fashioned a menorah with seven branches.

Moses cried in amazement, "God showed me repeatedly how to make the menorah, yet I could not properly get the idea; but you, without even having it shown to you by God, have made it so skillfully. Truly, you deserve the name Bezalel, which means 'in the shadow of God,' for you act as if you had been all the while in his shadow when he was showing me how to make the menorah." And ever since that time, the menorah has had the distinctive shape that was fashioned by Bezalel.

One Thing More in the Stocking
United States

Before telling this story, find a large, colorful Christmas stocking, one that has a seam at the toe. Carefully open up a part of the seam, and then "mend" the hole by running a piece of strong thread of the same color as the stocking around the hole, on the inside. Pull the ends of the thread tight, but do not tie them. Leave one end of the thread on the outside. Make sure it is long enough to grasp firmly. Then collect the items needed to fill the stocking, as described in the story below, and a small canvas bag to put them in. Find a place to hang the stocking *firmly* near the spot where you will stand or sit when telling the story.

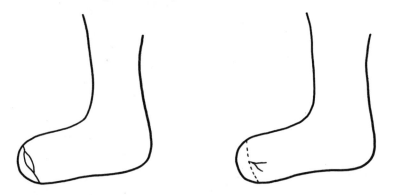

One Christmas Eve, Santa Claus came to a certain house to fill a child's stocking. It was hanging from the edge of the fireplace mantel. When Santa went up close to it, what should he see but—a little mouse.

"Merry Christmas, little friend," said Santa.

"The same to you, Santa," answered the mouse. "Do you mind if I stay and watch you for a while?"

"Not at all," said Santa. "Stay and watch as long as you like." So the mouse watched as Santa took gifts from his sack. He began to fill the stocking. First he put in an orange; then some Play-Doh; a box of crayons; a pair of socks; a mysterious box! He filled the stocking almost to the top and last of all, he stuffed in a small fuzzy_____. **(Use whatever stuffed animal you can find that will fit in the stocking and peek over the top.)**

"There, now it won't hold another thing!" said Santa with pride. "There is not a chink of space from top to toe."

The mouse's eyes twinkled beadily. "I know it's not polite to contradict, so I beg your pardon, but I must tell you, *I* could put one thing more in that stocking," squeaked the mouse.

"Ho, ho!" laughed Santa. "You silly mouse. Do you think I don't know how to pack? After all these years of filling stockings, I think I've acquired the knack of doing it well." He pointed to the stocking. "Put in one more thing—just one. I give you permission to try it." The mouse went right to the toe of the stocking. He nibbled and gnawed, nibbled and gnawed . . . **(At this point, pull the end of the thread or yarn. Keep repeating the above phrase, pretending you are gnawing at the toe, until the thread is pulled out and the hole shows.)** . . . until

he had made a big hole!

"I ask you, Santa, was that hole there before? Did I or did I not put one thing more in that stocking?" squeaked the mouse.

Santa Claus laughed. "That was a fine joke on me," he said, "and for that, little mouse, I shall give you a present, too." **(Reach into sack again and pull out a piece of cheese shaped like a Christmas cookie.)**

The Twelve Gifts of Christmas
Denmark, Sweden

Almost everyone is familiar with the old English carol "The Twelve Days of Christmas." What is not as widely known is the fact that in the Scandinavian countries there exists a song that is just as old as the English carol, possibly older. Most often called "Juledagsgave," it tells of the gifts a wealthy landowner gives to his servant on the twelve days of Christmas. If your audience has many small children, try using felt figures to accompany the chant.

Almost without trying, this is likely to become an audience participation story. However, to get the audience started, pause at the end of the first line in each couplet. They will usually supply the silly names. Try to say the last sequence very quickly.

There was once a young man who worked for a very rich landowner. The young man worked well for many years, but he never got paid by the master. He was just about to complain, when the rich man said, "This Christmas, I shall reward you for your long years of service."

On the first day of Christmas,
the young man got a hen.
He called his hen,

Tilleri-ten.
On the second day of Christmas, he got a rooster.
He called his rooster,
Out-of-bed-booster.
He called his hen,
Tilleri-ten.
On the third day of Christmas, he got a duck.
He called his duck,
Just-my-luck!
He called his rooster,
Out-of-bed-booster.
He called his hen,
Tilleri-ten.
On the fourth day of Christmas, he got a goose.
He called his goose,
Long-necked-and-loose.
He called his duck,
Just-my-luck!
He called his rooster,
Out-of-bed-booster.
He called his hen,
Tilleri-ten.
On the fifth day of Christmas, he got a goat.
He called his goat,
Trip-trap-shaggy-coat.
He called his goose,
Long-necked-and-loose.
He called his duck,
Just-my-luck!

He called his rooster,
Out-of-bed-booster.
He called his hen,
Tilleri-ten.
On the sixth day of Christmas, he got a cow.
He called his cow,
Milk-me-now!
He called his goat,
Trip-trap-shaggy-coat.
(Repeat sequence of goose, duck, rooster, hen.)
On the seventh day of Christmas, he got a pig.
He called his pig,
Oh-so-big!
He called his cow,
Milk-me-now!
(Repeat sequence of goat, goose, duck, rooster, hen.)
On the eighth day of Christmas, he got an ox.
He called his ox,
Horns-on-a-box.
He called his pig,
Oh-so-big!
(Repeat sequence of cow, goat, goose, duck, rooster, hen.)
On the ninth day of Christmas, he got a horse.
He called his horse,
Trot, of course!
He called his ox,
Horns-on-a-box.
(Repeat sequence of pig, cow, goat, goose, duck, rooster, hen.)
On the tenth day of Christmas, he got a cat.

He called his cat,
Furry-and-fat.
He called his horse,
Trot, of course!
He called his ox,
Horns-on-a-box.
(Repeat sequence of pig, cow, goat, goose, duck, rooster, hen.)
On the eleventh day of Christmas, he got a house.
He called his house,
Snug-as-a-mouse.
He called his cat,
Furry-and-fat.
He called his horse,
Trot, of course!
He called his ox,
Horns-on-a-box.
(Repeat sequence of pig, cow, goat, goose, duck, rooster, hen.)
On the twelfth day of Christmas, he married a wife.
He called his wife,
Joy-of-my-life.
He called his house,
Snug-as-a-mouse.
He called his cat,
Furry-and-fat.
He called his horse,
Trot, of course!
He called his ox,
Horns-on-a-box.
He called his pig,

Oh-so-big!
He called his cow,
Milk-me-now!
He called his goat,
Trip-trap-shaggy-coat.
He called his goose,
Long-necked-and-loose.
He called his duck,
Just-my-luck!
He called his rooster,
Out-of-bed-booster.
He called his hen,
Tilleri-ten.
Hen, rooster, duck, goose, goat, and cow,
Pig, ox, horse, cat, house, and spouse—
They all wish you a Merry Christmas!

The Groundhog Family
Ojibwa people of North America

This fable can be used on or near February 2, Groundhog Day. Another name for the groundhog is woodchuck. The Ojibwa word for it is *akukojeesh.*

A mother groundhog snuggled into her burrow one winter and there she stayed and hibernated with her children. Even though her burrow was long and had many compartments, she kept her little ones close to

her so they would stay warm. Every now and then she would go out and search for roots for them to eat. But she always warned them to stay deep inside the burrow and not go near the entrance.

The baby groundhogs listened to her and obeyed, but toward the end of winter they got impatient. They were tired of being cooped up in their cramped hole. Every day they would ask their mother, "Is it spring yet?" And she would always say, "No, no. Keep quiet. Wait here. It is still snowing and blowing out there."

One day she was gone a long time. Finally, she crept back into the burrow and fell into an exhausted sleep. The little groundhogs were suspicious. They took a peek at their mother, sleeping with her mouth open. On her lips and teeth they saw white specks. They looked closer. Yes, those were the remains of the roots from a dogtooth violet. To groundhogs, those were the best-tasting roots of all.

"She has deceived us," said the children. "It *is* spring." And they scampered out of the burrow and went off into the forest. From then on, they looked for their own food.

The mother groundhog awoke and smiled to see her children gone. She had not deceived them. She had protected them and kept them safe from harm until she knew there were enough roots growing for them to find easily and feed themselves.

Now, you may have heard the story about the groundhog and its shadow. On February 2, when the groundhog comes out of its burrow, it may be looking for its shadow. But most of all it is looking for the first signs of the dogtooth violet. If it finds no signs of that plant growing, it returns to the burrow to tell the groundhog children that spring will come a bit later that year.

Stories to memorize

Many handbooks of storytelling technique warn the teller not to memorize. On the other hand, a few of them mention it as a technique that some people find useful when learning a story. Some of the school contests and festivals of storytelling *insist* that the student performers memorize their stories. The organizers explain that they want young people to be aware of certain language patterns and they feel the best way to achieve that awareness is through story memorization.

For most folktales, it is probably better if the teller memorizes only a few key words and phrases, and the basic sequence of actions. Folktales are usually best when put into the teller's own words. But it is not a good idea to mix modern expressions with older forms of language, unless one is doing a parody. Try to keep to a consistent style of language.

There are some writers who have composed stories in a folktale or fairy-tale style. A few of these writers are Hans Christian Andersen, Rudyard Kipling, Howard Pyle, Carl Sandburg, and Eleanor Farjeon. Their stories have such unique language and style that it does not seem right to change any of the words when telling the stories. These stories must be memorized in order to have their best effect. But they must be memorized in such a way that the telling seems natural and effortless, as though one were using one's own words.

Another type of story that should be memorized is the parody. More than half of the young tellers I contacted for this book said they had told at least one story that was a takeoff on some famous story. This seems to be a favorite story type for young storytellers and listeners. Among the versions they had told were James Marshall's modern "Goldilocks and the Three Bears," "The Three Little Wolves and the Big Bad Pig," and a rap version of "Rapunzel."

The Lady's Room; a story by Eleanor Farjeon
England

Notice that the author wrote this in the form of a traditional chain tale. There is quite a bit of repetition, but there is also more description than in many folktales. Visualize the rooms in the order given: walls and ceiling first, then curtains, carpet, bed, and coverlet. Add the colors: white, green, pink, golden, and black. Before long each description will seem as familiar as your own room. The emphases are given here as the author wrote them. They should be given emphasis in the telling as well.

A lady once lived in a room that was as white as snow. Everything in it was white; it had white walls and ceiling, white silk curtains, a soft sheepskin carpet, and a little ivory bed with a white linen coverlet. The Lady thought it the most beautiful room in the world, and lived in it as happy as the day was long.

But one morning she looked out of the window and heard the birds singing in the garden, and all at once she sighed a big sigh.

"Oh, dear!"

"What's the matter with *you,* lady?" said a tiny voice at the window, and there, sitting on the sill, was a fairy no bigger than your finger, and on her feet she wore two little shoes as green as grass in April.

"Oh, fairy!" cried the lady, "I'm so tired of this plain white room! I would be so happy if it were only a green room!"

"*Right* you are, lady!" said the fairy, and she sprang on to the bed, and lay on her back, and kicked away at the wall with her two little feet. In the twinkling of an eye the white room turned into a green one, with green walls and ceiling, green net curtains, a carpet like moss in the woods, and a little green bed with a green linen coverlet.

"Oh, thank you, fairy!" cried the lady, laughing for joy. "Now I *shall* be as happy as the day is long!"

The fairy flew away, and the lady walked about her green room gay as a bird. But one day she looked out of the window and smelt the flowers growing in the garden, and all at once she began to sigh.

"Oh, dear! Oh, dear!"

"What's the matter with *you*, lady?" asked a tiny voice, and there on the windowsill sat the fairy, swinging her two little feet in shoes as pink as rose-petals in June.

"Oh, fairy!" cried the lady. "I made such a mistake when I asked you for a green room. I'm so tired of my green room! What I really meant to ask for was a pink room."

"*Right* you are, lady!" said the fairy, and jumped on the bed, and lay on her back, and kicked at the wall with her two little feet. All in a moment the green room changed into a pink one, with pink walls and ceiling, pink damask curtains, a carpet like rose-petals, and a little rosewood bed with a pink linen coverlet.

"Oh, thank you, fairy!" cried the lady, clapping her hands. "This is just the room I have always wanted!"

The fairy flew away, and the lady settled down in her pink room, as happy as a rose. But one day she looked out of her window and saw the leaves dancing in the garden, and before she knew it she was sighing like the wind.

"Oh, dear!" sighed the lady. "Oh, dear! Oh, dear!"

"What's the matter with *you*, lady?" cried the fairy's tiny voice, and there was the fairy hopping on the windowsill in a pair of shoes as golden as lime leaves in October.

"Oh, Fairy!" cried the lady. "I am so tired of my pink room! I can't think how I ever came to ask you for a pink room when all the time a golden room was what I really wanted."

"*Right* you are, Lady!" said the fairy, and she leaped on to the bed, lay on her back, and kicked at the wall with her two little feet. Quicker than you can wink, the pink room turned golden, with walls and ceiling like sunshine, and curtains like golden cobwebs, and a carpet like fresh-fallen lime leaves, and a little gold bed with a gold cloth coverlet.

"Oh, thank you, thank you!" cried the lady, dancing for joy. "At last I really have the very room I wanted!" The fairy flew away, and the lady ran around her golden room as lighthearted as a leaf. But one night she looked out of the window and saw the stars shining on the garden, and fell a-sighing, as though she would never stop.

"*Now* what's the matter with you, lady?" said the tiny voice from the windowsill. And there stood the fairy in a pair of shoes as black as night.

"Oh, Fairy!" cried the lady. "It is all this golden room! I cannot *bear* my bright golden room, and if only I can have a black room instead, I will never want any other as long as I live!"

"The matter with you, lady," said the fairy, "is that you don't know *what* you want!" And she jumped on the bed, and lay on her back, and kicked away with her two little feet. And the walls fell through, and the ceiling fell up, and the floor fell down, and the lady was left standing in the black starry night without any room at all.

The True Story of Jack and Jill
England

This parody could be used for a high school class in forensics or speech. While it would not be necessary to memorize all of it word for word, the ridiculously pompous and scholarly phrases should be used as they stand.

Etymological sagacity will enable us to interpret without difficulty the well-known myth of Jack as Hellenic in origin. It has reached us only in an English translation or adaptation. The key is at once found when we recognize in the name Jack the Greek Iacchus, a sun god. As the myth itself clearly shows, Iacchus (or Jack) does not stand for Phoebus Apollo, the midday sun. He is rather the morning and evening sun, the Red Sun of sunrise and sunset. In another of the Jack cycle of myths, this solar hero is a slayer of giants.

The climbing of the hill by Jack is nothing but the rising of the sun, and his subsequent fall is the setting of the sun. We need not account for the hill by supposing that the story assumed its present shape in some district where a level plain is bounded by hills, for in another myth it is not a hill but a beanstalk that is climbed by Jack. Thus it is the ascension, or

sun rising, not the thing ascended, on which the mythopoeic instinct has fastened.

The pail of water symbolizes the bright daylight fetched or restored by the sun. The cleansing or brightening properties of water, especially in pails, were well known to the Greeks.

The female associate of Jack is Jill, the morning or evening twilight, the light that precedes the rising and follows the setting of Jack, the Red Sun. Here again, etymology, properly applied, is conclusive. Jill or Gill is merely a short form of Gillette, the razor blade. In early days of metallurgy the resemblance between the bright blade and the steel blue light that precedes the dawn could not fail to strike the observer.

We must bear in mind that we possess the myth only in a late, literary, and translated form. Originally there can be no doubt that Jill, the twilight, went up the hill before Jack. This point has been somewhat obscured in the later tradition, but the lingering of the evening twilight after the setting of the Red Sun has fortunately been preserved. There remains to be accounted for the curious and enigmatic words " cracked his crown." The variant "broke his crown" may be confidently rejected, for early popular poetry is always alliterative. Reminding ourselves that we are dealing with an English translation of a Greek myth, the original of which has perished, we discover that at this point the Greek has been transliterated rather than translated. "Cracked his crown," stands for *ekraxen ho krounos,* or "the water hissed." When the red-hot ball of the setting sun appeared to dip in the sea, primitive Greek imagination heard the hissing sound that follows the dipping of red-hot metal into water.

This gives us, for the words, "Jack fell down and cracked his crown," the following interpretation: The Red Sun set and the water sizzled.

This entire explanation cannot fail to convince us by its very simplicity.

Master of All Masters
England

This appears to be so simple that one could tell it in one's own words. However, it works best when it is memorized, using no additional words. Because young children do not know that long ago people did not look for jobs the way we do now, I often introduce this story with a short explanation such as this: In olden days, when people wanted a job, they would go to the nearest big town on a day when a fair was going to take place. Fairs in those days were not like state fairs today. Instead, they served many of the same purposes as our malls of today, only they were outside. There was usually one spot where persons interested in being hired as servants or farm laborers would gather. Fairs were held only a few times each year, usually at the time of big religious holidays.

Carefully control your voice when speaking the lines of the young servant. Try to show eager interest at first, then mild interest, slight annoyance, greater annoyance, then finally total exasperation. Be sure to take a deep, obvious breath before saying the long sentence at the end. Say it as quickly as you can, but get all the words correct.

A girl once went to the fair to hire herself out as a servant. At last a funny-looking gentleman engaged her, and took her home to his house. When he got there, he told her he had some things to teach her, for in his house he had his own names for things.

He pointed to the bed. "What will you call that?"

"Bed, or cot, or whatever you please, sir," said the servant.

"No, that's my barnacle," said he.

He pointed to his trousers. "What will you call these?"

"Pants, or breeches, or whatever you please, sir," said she.

"You must call them squibs and crackers," said he.

"He pointed to the cat. "What will you call her?"

"Cat, or kitty, or whatever you please, sir," said she.

"You must call her white-faced simminy," said he.

He pointed to the fire. "What would you call this?"

"Fire, or flame, or whatever you please, sir," said she.

"You must call it hot cockalorum," said he.

He pointed to the water. "What will you call that?"

"Water, or wet, or whatever you please, sir," said she.

"No, pondalorum is its name," said he.

He pointed to the house all around him. "What will you call this?"

"House, or cottage, or whatever you please, sir," said she.

"You must call it high topper mountain," said he.

He pointed to himself. "What will you call me?"

"Master, or mister, or whatever you please, sir," said she.

"You must call me master of all masters," said he.

That very night, the servant woke her master in a fright and said—"Master of all masters get out of your barnacle and put on your squibs and crackers for white-faced simminy has got a spark of hot cockalorum on her tail and unless you get some pondalorum high topper mountain will be all on hot cockalorum."

Stories composed or improvised
by young people

Perhaps you enjoy writing parodies of well-known fairy tales. In that case you will probably enjoy the version of "Rapunzel" given here. Sometimes you may be given an assignment to do such a story for a writing class, and you may like the result so much you start to tell it to your friends. In other cases, it is a question of improvising the story at the moment of telling.

Or perhaps you enjoy making up entirely new tales, not based on any fairy-tale models. A type of story that I found making the rounds among groups of young people was the "trick" story, especially one using an object, like "The Fisherman's Surprise" (see page 61). Sometimes the trick story involved pinching or even spitting! Some stories from my own books came back to me in new forms. On a visit to Pleasant View School, near Antigo, Wisconsin, I found that children in all grades from one to six had invented variations on the string stories I wrote down in *The Story Vine*. A few of them had created entirely new stories, funny and clever and full of local color. If you invent an interesting story, send it to me in care of Simon & Schuster Books for Young Readers, 1230 Avenue of the Americas, New York, New York 10020.

Language Power
Mexican-American

While I was visiting the Lynn/Urquides School in Tucson, Arizona, the school suffered a breakdown of its water and power facilities. As I waited with some of the fifth graders for the problem to be solved, we shared a number of stories. Timmy G. was especially funny as he told several trick stories that involved rubbing or pinching his arms. This story was told in pieces by the whole group. They had heard it in their class the previous year, but could not remember from whom. The school is made up mostly of children of Mexican-American backgrounds. Many of them are of Yaqui heritage.

A family of barn mice decided to go exploring out into the wide world. The oldest mouse went off to the garden. He heard an owl hoot, "Who, who, who?" The mouse understood that language and scuttled back home.

The middle mouse went off down the road in front of the barn. All of a sudden, from overhead, he heard a shrieking scream from a hawk. He understood that language and rushed to get back to his home in the barn. The youngest mouse was small. She didn't venture too far— just into the hayloft. She made a rustling noise as she passed through the hay.

"Meow," said a purring voice. "Who's there? I know someone's hiding in the hay. Who is it?"

Youngest mouse opened her mouth as wide as she could and said

"Bowwow!" Then she scampered back down the mousehole to her family. When the mice told their mother about their adventures, she said, "You see, I told you it would come in handy. Now, aren't you glad I'm raising you to be bilingual?"

The Continued Adventures of Rapunzel
United States

Many young people like to take one of the standard folktales and adapt it in some way. The Traveling Storytellers of Conneaut Carnegie Library in Conneaut, Ohio, were a group of teenagers who performed in their area. One of the stories they told was a "rap" version of "Rapunzel." To accompany that story, they composed this tale. It is reprinted here with their permission.

Because of the "library" theme, this would be appropriate for telling during National Library Week. In that case, be sure to have a large version of the international sign for *library* and hold it up to the audience at the appropriate time in the story.

You've heard the story of Rapunzel and her golden braid and how her tears restored the blind Prince's eyesight. But, do you know what happened next? Sit back, relax, and listen.

The Prince and Rapunzel were married. It was a small, informal affair. You see, Rapunzel was a peasant, the daughter of a witch, and the Prince's family did not approve of her. They disowned him. Now, that means he wasn't allowed to come to the family castle and he certainly wasn't rich anymore. Rapunzel didn't mind being poor. She and the Prince were in love. They lived in a hut in the forest.

One day a messenger came to their little hut in the forest. He announced, "The witch is dead. It was stated in her will that upon her death this chest was to be delivered to Rapunzel." Then he gave her an old leather chest.

After the messenger left, Rapunzel opened the chest and found her golden braid that the witch had chopped off in the tower. When Rapunzel took the braid out, it unwound and a book fell to the floor. It was the witch's diary. She immediately sat down and started to read.

Hours of reading and many tears later, she called to her husband, "Prince, come here! You'll never believe what I have discovered. The witch was not my mother. My parents were neighbors of the witch. They had another daughter. I have a sister. Her name is Jorinda."

Tragically, both her parents had died from eating too much rampion, a lettuce-type vegetable that you-know-who was named after. All her life, in her heart, Rapunzel had felt that the witch was not her mother and she had always longed for a sister.

She and the Prince began searching for her sister Jorinda. They traveled from town to town throughout Germany. Finally, in a small village, the international sign for libraries led them to the local library. They went inside to check the newspapers for any information. There they found that Jorinda had worked as the children's librarian. They also discovered that two brothers by the name of Jacob and Wilhelm Grimm also had worked in the library and that Jorinda had fallen in love with Wilhelm. The Grimm brothers were collecting folktales for a book that they planned to write one day. Just the week before, they had gone to America and Jorinda went with them.

"Please, Prince," begged Rapunzel. "May we go to America to find my sister?"

"You have no family here in Germany. My family has disowned me. Why not? Yes, let's go to America," declared the Prince.

Rapunzel and the Prince boarded a ship bound for America. It was a long, hard voyage but at last they landed at Ellis Island in New York. Before entering America, they were asked many questions.

"And what is your last name?" an immigration clerk asked the couple.

"Oh, we have no last names. I'm Rapunzel and this is my husband, the Prince," said Rapunzel.

"You must have last names in America," said the clerk.

The two talked it over and decided to take the last name of Unzel. So, they became the Prince and Princess Unzel.

That taken care of, they began searching all over New York City for Jorinda. Again, the international sign for libraries led them to a library. They went inside thinking that perhaps the threesome might be found or have library cards there. Rapunzel was discussing her search for her long-lost sister named Jorinda with a library clerk, when a beautiful girl with a long blond braid said, "Excuse me, but my name is Jorinda and I'm from Germany!"

Rapunzel told Jorinda her tale. The two cried, they hugged, and they laughed. Jorinda brought the Prince and Rapunzel to her apartment in a part of New York known as Queens. The Grimm brothers were living in the apartment next door. Jorinda and Rapunzel repeated their story to the brothers.

"That is a very good story. We may write that down someday and add it to the tales in our book," said the Brothers Grimm.

To make a long story short, the Grimm brothers decided to return to Germany to continue their work of collecting German folktales. But before they left New York City, they wrote the story of Rapunzel and gave it to the Prince and his wife. Jorinda decided to stay in New York City for a while before returning to Germany.

The Prince and Rapunzel had many children. Each night, before bed, they would read the Grimm brothers' story of Rapunzel. The reading became a tradition in the Unzel family and to this day Unzel children are still hearing the story. The brothers also wrote a story for Jorinda called "Jorinda and Joringel." These and many more stories can be found at the Conneaut Carnegie Library and libraries all over the world.

The Tofu's Illness
Japan

This story is the result of the collaboration of Aya Nagashima, Myonha So, and Junko Tsukiyama, three first graders in Koka Gakuen, a school in Tokyo. They were asked to compose a story in the folktale tradition.

Tofu is soybean curd. If you are telling this to little children, it might be a good idea to have some tofu and one of each of the vegetables mentioned to show before the story starts.

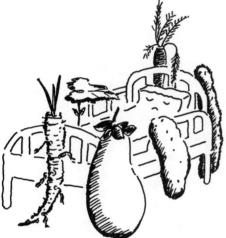

One day Tofu got sick and had to go to the hospital. White Radish powdered her face and said she was going to visit Tofu. She went to the other vegetables and asked them if they would come along with her. But they all refused to come and each one gave a reason.

"I have been bitten by insects and I am full of a rash," said Cucumber.

"I got a sunburn," said Carrot.

"I fell down and bruised myself until I'm black and blue," said Eggplant.

"I, too, fell down but my skin just got dented in a lot of places," said Potato.

"I am busy mending the roof of my house, and I am covered with a layer of dust," said Burdock Leaf.

So White Radish went off to visit Tofu alone. But Tofu was still lonely, so he said to White Radish, "Go back and tell them they can visit me just as they are. I won't mind."

White Radish returned to the vegetables and they came to visit Tofu just as they were: Cucumber with a prickly rash, Carrot with a sunburn, Eggplant all black and blue, Potato full of dents, and Burdock Leaf with a fine covering of dust. And from then on they stayed that way, and that is why these vegetables are the way they are.

The Storyteller; a poem by Rebecca Stallings
United States

Rebecca has been telling stories since she was ten, but she wrote this poem at age seventeen. "The Squire's Bride," the story mentioned in her poem, is found in Nordic folklore. The best-known version can be found in *Norwegian Folktales* by Peter C. Asbjornsen and Jorgen Moe.

Her heart quickens at the sight of the empty stage
And of the audience—
At least a hundred people, and she is only one.
They are waiting, hushed, ready . . .
No turning back. She walks onto the stage,
Her smile confident above the quivering heart.
How does it begin?
Push the first words through the panic.
"Once, long ago in Europe, there lived a very rich man."
The story begins, a few tenuous sentences
Extending like glittering threads.
Eye contact—
There! The little boy in the third row
Catches hold of a silver strand of story
Delicate as a spiderweb. She watches him
As the story spins on,
Weaving sentences from thin air.
Gestures flow through her arms; the words continue
Telling a story written by others, embroidered with details
From some untouched part of her mind.

People are laughing, not at her, not with her,
It's the story that tickles them as they await
The next clever line that slips out
Of nowhere, surprising her—did I say that?
The story is finished.
It floats in the air, perfect as a soap bubble
Swirled with the rainbow of everyone's dreams.
"And that's the story of 'The Squire's Bride.' "

Bibliography

Included here are books and other items used as the sources of the stories in this book, as well as books, manuals, guides, and the like referred to in part 1 and part 2. Individual stories are in the index by title and by author, if they have an author. By turning to the page on which the story is mentioned, you will find the book in which it can be found. Books and stories available in numerous editions, such as Kipling's *Just So Stories*, "The Three Little Pigs," and others of that kind are not included here, unless they are modern, copyrighted versions such as James Marshall's *Goldilocks and the Three Bears*. The books marked with an asterisk (*) include many other stories that young people enjoy telling or hearing.

Aardema, Verna. *Who's in Rabbit's House?* New York: Dial, 1977.

Almario, Virgilio S. *The Trial of the Animals.* London: Methuen, 1983.

Arvidsson, A. I. *Svenska Fornsånger.* Vol. 3. Stockholm: P. A. Norstedt, 1842.

*Asbjornsen, Peter C. and Jorgen Moe. *Norwegian Folktales.* New York: Viking, 1960.

*Bauer, Carolyn Feller. *The New Storyteller's Handbook.* Chicago: American Library Association, 1993.

Bellman, Beryl, and Jules-Rosette Bennetta. *A Paradigm for Looking.* Norwood, N.J.: Ablex, 1977.

*Belpre, Pura. *The Tiger and the Rabbit and Other Tales.* Philadelphia: Lippincott, 1944.

Bleek, W. H. I. *Reynard the Fox in South Africa.* London: Trubner, 1864.

*Bronner, Simon J. *American Children's Folklore.* Little Rock: August House, 1988.

*Brunvand, Jan Harold. *The Baby Train.* New York: W. W. Norton, 1993.

*———. *The Choking Doberman.* New York: W. W. Norton, 1984.

*———. *The Vanishing Hitchhiker.* New York: W. W. Norton, 1981.

Carvajal, Julio E., and Silvia A. Dellepiane. *Para Escuchar, Decir y Cantar: Folklore

Aplicada en el Jardin de Infantes. Buenos Aires: Editorial Plus Ultra, 1988.

*Chase, Richard. *Grandfather Tales.* Boston: Houghton Mifflin, 1948.

*Courlander, Harold. *The Tiger's Whisker and Other Tales and Legends from Asia and the Pacific.* New York: Harcourt Brace, 1959.

*Farjeon, Eleanor. *The Little Bookroom.* London: Oxford University Press, 1955.

Feilberg, Henning F., comp. *Jul.* 2 vols. Copenhagen: Det Schubotheske, 1904.

*Fowke, Edith. *Folklore of Canada.* Toronto: McClelland & Stewart, 1976.

Galdone, Joanna. *The Tailypo, a Ghost Story.* Boston: Clarion, 1984.

Gask, Lilian. *Folk Tales from Many Lands.* London: George G. Harrap, 1910.

Ginzberg, Louis. *Legends of the Jews.* Vol. 3. Philadelphia: Jewish Publication Society, 1911.

Guirao, Ramón. *Cuentos y leyendas negras de Cuba.* Havana: Ediciones Mirador, 1942.

Hamilton, Martha, and Mitch Weiss. *Children Tell Stories.* Katonah, N.Y.: Richard C. Owen Publishers, 1990.

*Hamilton, Virginia. *The People Could Fly.* New York: Knopf, 1985.

*Jacobs, Joseph. *English Folk and Fairy Tales.* New York: Putnam, n.d.

Junion Storyteller: A Newletter for Young Storytellers. Masonville, CO: Storycraft Publishing, quarterly.

Kristensen, Ewald. *Danske Børnerim, Remser og Lege.* Aarhus, Denmark: K. Schonberg, 1896.

———. *Danske Dyrefabler og Kjaederemser.* Aarhus, Denmark: K. Schonberg, 1896.

Lederbogen, Wilhelm. *Duala Märchen.* Berlin: Mittheilungen des Seminars für Orientalische Sprachen, Abteilung 3, 1901.

Livo, Norma, and Sandra A. Rietz. *Storytelling Activities.* Littleton, Colo.: Libraries Unlimited, 1987.

Maas, Selva. *The Moon Painters and Other Estonian Folktales.* New York: Viking, 1971.

*MacDonald, Margaret Read. *Look Back and See.* New York: H. W. Wilson, 1991.

*————. *Peace Tales: World Folktales to Talk About.* Hamden, Conn.: Linnet Books, 1992.

*————. *The Storyteller's Start-up Book.* Little Rock: August House, 1993.

*————. *Twenty Tellable Tales.* New York: H. W. Wilson, 1986.

Marshall, James. *Goldilocks and the Three Bears.* New York: Dial, 1988.

*Miller, Teresa, comp., with assistance from Anne Pellowski. *Joining In.* Cambridge, Mass.: Yellow Moon Press, 1988.

Munsch, Robert. *50 Below Zero.* Toronto: Annick Press, 1986.

National Storytelling Directory. Jonesborough, Tenn.: National Storytelling Assoc., annual.

New York Public Library. *Stories: A List of Stories to Tell and Read Aloud.* 8th ed. New York: Office of Branch Libraries, New York Public Library, 1990.

Norlind, Tobias. *Svenska Allmogens Lif.* Stockholm: Bohlen, 1912.

*Pellowski, Anne. *The Family Storytelling Handbook.* New York: Macmillan, 1987.

*————. *Hidden Stories in Plants.* New York: Macmillan, 1990.

*————. *The Story Vine.* New York: Macmillian, 1984.

*————. *A World of Children's Stories.* New York: Friendship Press, 1993.

————. *The World of Storytelling.* Rev. ed. New York: H. W. Wilson, 1990.

*Richardson, Frederick. *Great Children's Stories.* New York: Hubbard, 1972.

*Robinson, Adjai. *Singing Tales of Africa.* New York: Scribner's, 1974.

San Souci, Robert, and Jerry Pinkney. *The Talking Eggs.* New York: Dial, 1989.

*Schimmel, Nancy. *Just Enough to Make a Story.* Rev. ed. San Francisco: Sister's Choice Press, 1987.

Schoolcraft, Henry Rowe. *The Myth of Hiawatha and Other Oral Legends.* Philadelphia: Lippincott, 1856.

*Serwadda, Moses, and Hewitt Pantaleoni. *Songs and Stories from Uganda.* New York: Thomas Y. Crowell, 1974.

*Shaphard, Robert, and James Thomas, comp. *Sudden Fiction.* Salt Lake City: Gibbs M. Smith, 1986.

*———. *Sudden Fiction International.* New York: W. W. Norton, 1989.

Tremearne, A. J. N. *Hausa Superstitions and Customs.* London: J. Bale, 1913.

*Walker, Barbara. *The Dancing Palm Tree and Other Nigerian Tales.* New York: Parents Magazine Press, 1968. Reprint, Lubbock, Tex: Texas Tech University Press, 1990.

Wells, Rosemary. *Max's Christmas.* New York: Dial, 1986.

When the Troupe Tells Tales. Videotape of the Roosevelt Middle School Tellers. 49 min. 1993. Produced by Robert Rubinstein, 90 East 49th Ave., Eugene, OR 97405.

*Withers, Carl. *I Saw a Rocket Walk a Mile.* New York: Holt Rinehart, 1965.

*Wolkstein, Diane. *The Magic Orange Tree.* New York: Schocken, 1980.

———. *Squirrel's Song, a Hopi Indian Tale.* New York: Knopf, 1976.

Sources of the Stories

"The Alligator's Whistle"
Both the music and the text for this story are my translation and adaptation of stories and songs found in Ramón Guirao's *Cuentos y leyendas negras de Cuba.*

"The Ant and the Grasshopper"
This is adapted from the verse version printed in *Bewick's Select Fables of Aesop,* which was a reprint combining many of the Aesop editions illustrated by the famous eighteenth-century wood engraver, Thomas Bewick.

"The Bar of Gold"
I based this on a short oral summary by Hans Halbey of Mainz, Germany, and on the printed version found in Lilian Gask's *Folk Tales from Many Lands*. Other versions can be found in Julia Cowles's *Art of Storytelling*, in Carolyn Sherwin Bailey's *Tell Me Another Story*, and in Minna B. Noyes's *Twilight Tales*. An Asian version is in Arthur B. Chrisman's *Treasures Long Hidden*.

"The Bear and the Seven Little Children"
More than twenty years ago I attended the Toronto Storytelling Festival for the first time. During the open storytelling session, when anyone from the audience could get up and tell a story, someone told a version of this tale. I heard the name Ruth Rubin and mistakenly assumed the teller was Ruth Rubin, an eminent ethnomusicologist whose family was of Polish-Jewish background but lived in Canada at the time. I began telling the story in my own way, adding the use of nesting dolls. I also added the Hanukkah element when telling it at holiday time. Only many years later did I find out that the very young teller at the Toronto Festival was not Ruth Rubin! I also found a printed version of Ms. Rubin's story in Edith Fowke's *Folklore of Canada*, and realized that I had changed the story quite a bit. However, I still like to say that the story comes from Ruth Rubin, because her version contains the delightful motif of the children hiding from the bear, which makes it so distinctive from the"Wolf and the Seven Little Kids"variant.

"The Continued Adventures of Rapunzel"
Reprinted here with the permission of The Traveling Storytellers of Conneaut Carnegie Library, Conneaut, Ohio, and the permission of their library adviser and leader, Stephanie Gildone.

"The Fisherman's Surprise"
This story is repeated here, with only slight changes, as it was told to me by Melissa McCulloch at Eric Smith School in Ramsey, New Jersey.

"The Glutton"
Hundreds of *ekaki uta* (drawing songs) have been collected from children in Japan. This one can be found in numerous printed versions. Satoshi Kako's *Nihon Densho No Asobi Tokumon* and Fumio Koizumi's *Kodomo no asobi to uta* together include almost a dozen variants. These were roughly translated by Shigeo Watanabe, and from the rough translations

I created this version. Shigeo Watanabe and I are working on a collection of drawing stories for children from Japan and other countries.

"The Groundhog Family"
I have been telling this ever since I first discovered, in the early 1960s, the work of Henry Rowe Schoolcraft. Starting in the early nineteenth century, he began recording tales, myths, customs, and other information about various Algonquian-speaking groups with which he came in contact. His wife was half Ojibwa, so his work among that group (sometimes known as Ojibway or Chippewa) was made easier for him. This tale can be found in his book *The Myth of Hiawatha and Other Oral Legends*.

"The King's Diamond Cross"
This appears in a verse version in *St. Nicholas Magazine*, February 1904, as written by Mrs. Frank Lee. Although I have used early issues of *St. Nicholas Magazine* for a number of stories in my repertoire, I had not come across this one until my attention was called to it by Barbara Snow of Eugene, Oregon. The text given here is as I now tell it.

"The Lady's Room"
Reprinted from *The Little Bookroom* by Eleanor Farjeon

"Language Power"
One of the Tucson schools I visited as part of a Library Power (Reader's Digest/Dewitt Jones) grant was the Lynn/Urquides School. This story was told in snatches by a group of fifth graders. I re-created it in my own words from my brief notes (a total of seventeen words!).

"Little Chick with the Dirty Beak"
This is my own translation and version of a story I have heard in a number of South and Central American countries. The easiest-to-tell Spanish version can be found in *Para Escuchar, Decir y Cantar: Folklore Aplicada en el Jardin de Infantes* by Julio E. Carvajal and Silvia A. Dellepiane, distributed in the U.S. by Bilingual Publications Company, 270 Lafayette Street, New York, NY 10012.

"The Little Girl and Her Oninga"
This is my own adaptation of the story as it appears in W. H. I. Bleek's *Reynard the Fox in South Africa*. I could not find an equivalent English name for the fruit mentioned there, so I substituted *oninga*, the Herero word for "plum."

118

"Master of All Masters"
This old "droll" is reprinted from *English Folk and Fairy Tales* by Joseph Jacobs. I have made only minor changes, chiefly in the order in which the "master" asks the questions. I have always found it more dramatic to have the question "What will you call me?" put at the end of the series. Put it back as the first question if you prefer to keep the order the same as in the final sentence.

"The Noisy Gecko"
I have frequently used the picture book *The Trial of the Animals,* which is a Filipino version of this tale. The Indonesian version I learned during a storytelling and bookmaking workshop in Jakarta in October 1993. Mrs. Toety Maklis, one of the leading children's book writers in Indonesia, was especially helpful in writing down for me the phonetic spellings of the animal sounds.

"One Thing More in the Stocking"
This is adapted from a story in verse that appeared in the January 1884 issue of *St. Nicholas Magazine.* It was written by Emilie Poulsson and the title there was "Santa Claus and the Mouse."

"The Orphan Boy"
This is my own adaptation of a story recorded by Beryl Bellman and Jules-Rosette Bennetta when they were doing cross-cultural research with visual media in West Africa. The fascinating results of some of their research can be found in their book, *A Paradigm for Looking.* A short resume of this story can be found on page 41 in that book.

"Point of View"
While doing workshops in Ghana and Cameroon in 1988, I heard many stories. When trying to find variants, I came upon this tale in Wilhelm Lederbogen's *Duala Märchen.* This is basically a translation of that version, which seemed to be remarkably close to the way it would be told orally. The title is my invention.

"The Tofu's Illness"
This was submitted by the principal of the Shogakko (the primary division) at the Koka Gakuen School in Chofu-shi, Tokyo, and translated into English by Kiyoko Toyama. I polished the translation and put it into tellable English.

"The True Story of Jack and Jill"
Slightly adapted and abridged from *Cornhill Magazine,* January 1914. The author is given only the initials M. M.

"The Twelve Gifts of Christmas"
Many years ago Knud Eigil Hauberg-Tychsen of Copenhagen sang for me a few verses of this song, in Danish. We had been discussing drawing songs, story songs, stories in string, and other types of stories that rarely get written down. My research took me into numerous old nineteenth-century and early twentieth-century collections from Denmark, Norway, and Sweden. Among those sources were two books by Ewald Kristensen, *Danske Dyrefabler og Kjaederemser* and *Danske Børnerim, Remser og Lege;* two volumes of *Jul,* collected by Henning F. Feilberg; A. I Arvidsson's *Svenska Fornsånger;* and Tobias Norlind's *Svenska Allmogens Lif.* Some scholars speculate that this song is an offshoot of the very early Jewish song "One Little Goat," usually sung as part of Hanukkah celebrations. The translation here is my own, combining couplets from all of the versions I eventually located.

"Why the Menorah Has Its Distinctive Shape"
This is my retelling of the story as it is found in Louis Ginzberg's *Legends of the Jews,* volume 3.

Acknowledgments

"The Lady's Room" by Eleanor Farjeon, copyright 1955, Oxford University Press, reprinted by permission of David Higham Associates, London.

I would also like to thank the persons who shared with me their storytelling experiences. Here I can only cite those who took extra time in their busy schedules to give me an interview or who wrote down their comments and sent them to me. They are listed in alphabetical order by state.
Students at Lynn/Urquides School, Tucson, Arizona; Mary Lynne McGrath and students in Sacramento City Unified School District; Ruth Stotter, Dominican College, San Francisco; Larry Johnson, teacher, Sarah Burman and many other students at Pillsbury School, Minneapolis; Cheryl Sawyer, Coon Rapids, Minnesota; Lynn Rubright, Kirkwood, Missouri; Ruthilde Kronberg, Katherine Wittenberg, Mona Vespa, Christina Wiegand, and

Katie Vagnino, all from the St. Louis area; Shirley A. Keyser, teacher, and Melissa McCulloch, student, at Eric Smith School, Ramsey, New Jersey; Lucille Thomas and Diane Wolkstein of New York City; Beauty and the Beast (Martha Hamilton and Mitch Weiss) of Ithaca, New York; Stephanie Gildone, librarian, and Josh Williams, Jennifer Johnston, Sabrina Lane, Beth Simpson, Tammy Muchiarone, Katie Eble, Monice Ovenmaa, Melissa Allen, Michelle Ladara, Abby Laughlin, Marcy Chapman, Abbie Hamilton, Hattie Grubke, and Julie Moore of Conneaut, Ohio; Mike, Dave, and John Collard from the Cleveland, Ohio, area; Fran Stallings of Bartlesville, Oklahoma; Robert Rubinstein and the Troupe of Tellers, Eugene, Oregon; Barbara Snow of Eugene; Rebecca Stallings of Pittsburgh, Pennsylvania; Betsy Boyd of Houston, Texas; Margaret Read MacDonald and Meg, Jocelyn, and Dawn Lippert, all from the Seattle, Washington, area; Mary Briggs and Riza Falk of Cochrane/Fountain City High School, Wisconsin; Mrs. Jean Greenwood and daughter Molly of Merrill, Wisconsin; students and teachers at Pleasant View School, Antigo, Wisconsin; Jane K. of Milwaukee; Troop 339, Girl Scouts of Greater Milwaukee; Ruth Johnson, teacher, and many students at Sprucecourt School, Toronto, Canada; Betty Nicholas of Department of Defense Dependent Schools (DODDS), Wiesbaden, Germany; and the following students who participated in the 7th Storytelling Festival: Scott Fugal, Robert T. McKnight III, Lori Prince, Laura Macky, Marianne Kinney, and Vanessa Motley; Toety Maklis of Indonesia; Somboon Singkamanen of Thailand; Shigeo Watanabe, writer and translator, Tokyo; Kiyoko Toyama and students of Koka Gakuen, also from Tokyo. A special note of thanks to John Collard for the musical arrangement in "The Alligator's Whistle."